The Shape of Us

MARY ANN TIPPETT

"It is not in the stars to hold our destiny but in ourselves."
— William Shakespeare

"You can't see the world through a mirror."
— Avril Lavigne

chapter 1

THERE WAS NOT A SINGLE WEIGHT-LOSS OBSTACLE SUSAN SNOW COULDN'T SOLVE WITH A RECIPE. For picky eaters, she probed their list of likes and dislikes before getting to work on the perfect casserole. For juice cleansers struggling with rebound weight, she developed smoothies and soups to keep hunger at bay and metabolism humming. For go-all-day, no-time-to-eat types, she looked at their grab-and-go favorites and created easy, less damaging alternatives. And for the afternoon laggers who undid all their calorie-counting plans at three o'clock every day, her Crave-Killer Cookies usually did the trick.

She had a gift for recipe matching. It started when she saw her own weight creep up with each of her three children. The first two gave her five extra pounds she figured would disappear when she had time to set her mind to it. Caleb had kept his arms firmly around her when he wasn't screeching in horror at her audacity to pee in peace. And Kimberly had turned up her nose at anything not covered in a solid crust of deep-fried batter or cheese. Inventing recipes to insert the odd nutrient into Kim's mouth was an exhausting exercise that rarely delivered. But before Susan could get serious with her problem-solving, Ester came along and added three more pounds.

It was time to get down to business. Susan analyzed her routines and obstacles while the kids napped. She figured out the differences between her pre-child behaviors versus post-child. At night when the kids were in bed, she set to work cooking and baking, slowly building an arsenal of recipes that allowed her to approximate her old way of eating while appeasing Kimberly's pickiness and Caleb's insatiable appetite. After that, she started running at six o'clock every morning before the kids awoke. Between the new recipes and the running, which also provided the mental clarity she needed to stick with her plan, the eight pounds vanished.

Today, she was working on a bloat-free banana bread for one of her ShapeShifters members. This would be her fifth year working part-time for a weight-loss company. It was the only job she could find that accommodated her busy lifestyle once the kids were in school. She enjoyed helping others who struggled for control over their weight. And the program worked well. It worked even better for members who came to her with specific issues she could address with her recipe-matching gift. Every time she helped someone on this personal level, she knew she was in the right place. And now that the kids were mostly grown, she expected her track record would land her a promotion.

"Smells good!" Susan's husband called from the foyer. She sniffed at the toasted nut aroma of her banana bread, feeling pleased about the ad-libbed almond flour. Too many gluten-free recipes used rice flour, which was chalky at worst and tasteless at best. This was her third attempt at getting it right.

"It's sugar- and gluten-free." She washed the last mixing bowl and placed it on the drying rack. Lex wrapped his arms around her and kissed her neck. Usually he would comment on the no-this, no-that in her recipes. She turned to look into his tired, slightly glazed eyes. "What happened?" she asked.

"You don't want to know," Lex said.

Probably a fentanyl overdose, Susan thought. *Or another shooting.* They were lucky to live in a country where these unnecessary deaths were statistically low. But hospitals saw it all —many more incidents than reported in the newspapers. She couldn't help thinking of Ester and her growing inability to protect her daughter from the perils that befell teenagers more than other age groups.

She knew Ester was a good kid, but even the good ones showed up in the hospital morgues. Illegal guns and laced cocaine had rapidly replaced spiked drinks. Lex and his

ER staff were on the front lines as these senseless travesties screamed from the daily papers.

She watched Lex wander to the fridge and open the door. "A glutenous version is still in the oven," she said, pointing to a loaf cooling at the end of their long marble island. Lex cut off a slice and smiled appreciatively, pressing the whole thing into his mouth before slicing another.

"You must be hungry." She smiled, delighted he was enjoying her creation. "I'll warm up the chicken diablo."

"Mmmmm, my favorite," he said, snaking his arms around her again and pulling her close. She could feel the taut muscles in his arms loosening, the thump of his heart slowing where her head met his chest.

"Will you be able to sleep?" she asked. Her husband had a knack for separating the trauma of hospital work from his personal life; the veil of bloody horrors and pale, unblinking innocents dropped away whenever he entered their house. But every now and then, a patient would get to him, and shaking it off wasn't so easy. He rested his cheek against her hair, breathing in the botanical scent of her shampoo.

She felt him nod. "You went for a run?"

"I had the most frustrating new member."

He unwrapped his arms and took a seat at the island, keen to dive into a mundane topic. His eyes became hyper focused, relief washing over the muscles in his face. She grinned, knowing he looked forward to her stories. Distractions from more serious issues.

Susan pulled the casserole dish from the fridge. "This

woman walks in, first through the door as I'm just getting set up, and wants to lose five pounds. Who doesn't, right?"

The oven timer went off. Susan took out the loaf and set it on a cooling rack. Then she slid the casserole into the oven and reset the timer. "She's five-eight, long legs. What I wouldn't give for those legs! Full head of blond hair, like mine, but longer and less frizzy. She looks like a model compared to all the others. She walks in all entitled like she's consulting a personal dietician. Honestly, she seemed oblivious to the real-world suffering going on around her."

Lex smiled at this. "My beautiful wife. Saving the world, one obese case at a time."

Susan smacked him playfully on the arm. "I'm serious, though," she said, placing two wine glasses on the island. She poured from a bottle of buttery Chardonnay and sat beside him with her own plate. "We can't let obviously fit and trim people into the program, especially the obsessive compulsive ones."

"Why not?" he said, sipping the wine. "Great choice," he added. "The subtle acidity is perfect with the toffee sweetness in the banana bread."

Susan smiled at the compliment. "I knew you'd like it." Her smile turned into a frown. "It affects our stats, for one thing. There's a reason we're the number one weight-loss program in the province."

"You think she's anorexic?" Lex said, taking another sip.

"Well, no. Hard to say. But she doesn't belong in a ShapeShifters program. She probably just needs to change up her life. Find a sport. Get a hobby. I mean, five pounds!

You can lose and gain that much in a day, depending on what you eat, drink, and poop."

Lex laughed. "Sounds like you need to invite her on one of your runs." Before she could object to that idea, they were interrupted by the melodious notes of Susan's phone. Lex raised a brow. "'Eyes Without a Face'?"

Susan crossed to the counter where she dropped her purse after work, shaking her head. "Ester's always messing with it. It went off during my meeting last week blaring 'I like big butts … '" She looked at the incoming number and her stomach lurched. She picked up anyway. "Aunt Maggie, hi! Can I call you back? Just about to eat dinner." Susan gestured at Lex this-should-be-quick style.

"I know it was you who took it," said a craggy voice in response.

Susan glanced at Lex and gave him a weak smile. "You okay, Mags?" she said, grabbing three plates and rushing around the corner with them to the dining room.

"Don't change the subject. You said you saw it the day of the wake, and that's the last time anyone saw it."

"Are you talking about that mirror again?" Susan whispered, setting down the plates and heading to the farthest corner of the room away from the kitchen. "It's been ten years. If it's lost —"

"You know gosh darned well it's not lost," Aunt Maggie attempted to shout hoarsely. "You took it!"

Susan sighed. "I don't know why you keep blaming me for this unfortunate loss of yours, but I … Can we continue this conversation later, please? Ester will be home any minute, and I have to get dinner out of the oven."

"Tell me what you saw in it, then."

Susan stood there, paralyzed by the memory. She fought the lump in her throat, her head swelling with something like rage and sorrow combined. "It was an emotional day," she finally said and hung up.

"What was that about?" Lex set two water glasses on the table.

Susan switched off the sound to her phone and forced a smile. "She hasn't been the same since Dad died. Always going on about some inane thing or another." The oven timer sounded just as Ester struggled into the foyer with her field hockey gear.

chapter

2

SINCE SHE MOVED TO CANADA, ANGELA MARSHALL HAD GAINED EXACTLY FIVE POUNDS. That worked out to about a pound a month. What would happen if she kept that up? Unacceptable! "I'm here to lose five pounds." Angela rehearsed the words in the car on her way to the weight-loss center, mentally checking off the reasons for this drastic measure.

She had tried skipping breakfasts. That didn't work. She tried fasting. That just made her susceptible to cravings. She tried a liquids-only approach. That just got her drunk faster when she and Melvin headed out to the pubs. She even tried amping up her exercise. That just made her appetite stronger. All the strategies that worked for her back in Fairview crashed and burned here.

It can't be related to Mount Pleasant, she reasoned. The obese per capita ratio in her new hometown barely existed compared to the States. Never one for fad diets, she decided it came down to adapting. Something about Canadian living was foiling her.

When her stepson, Jeremy, requested a French tutor, Angela realized she needed help. The ShapeShifters sign shone like a beacon upon the grocery where she picked up some snackables one night. Intrigued, she did some googling. Lucky for her, the most convenient weight-loss business was also the most popular. She gave herself exactly one week to make peace with her five extra pounds before deciding fifty years old was too young for surrendering. If a high school boy could admit he needed help, what was she waiting for?

Having parked her car in the Spring Mill Mall lot, she rehearsed the words one more time in the rearview mirror. Admitting she needed help did not come easy. She did not need help getting into law school or passing the bar exam, after all. She did not need help with parenting. Becoming a stepmom to Jeremy came so easily, she often forgot he was born of another. Then again, the bar was pretty low after his mother remarried and moved away, leaving Jeremy's dad to solo parent.

She glanced just once at the curve of flesh against her belt, then did a mirror check. Why did her hair and makeup look so off when she felt fat? Surely that sort of thing was all in her head. *Well, here goes nothing.*

She walked through the doors next to a shawarma "We Also Do Pizza" restaurant, pausing by a broken elevator. Why was it legal to bake fresh pita next to the entranceway of a weight-loss center? Making a mental note to bring this up to the powers that be, and drawing in a deep, cleansing breath, she ascended one flight of stairs that felt like two. She gathered herself on the other side of a door at the top, panting heavily next to another woman doing the same. She checked the address at the end of a long, bleak hallway to make sure she was at the right place. *Here goes*, she thought and pushed open the pocked panel door.

Inside, she found a spectacle of chartreuse and pomegranate pink. From the wall of boxed edibles and cooking tools on her left, to the picture of a celebrity—she couldn't think just who—on her right, the walls and practically everything else blared perky green and pink. The "ShapeShifters" lettering on the opposite wall out-glared the other colors by adding neon light. Under the neon and across a small lobby in front of Angela stood a waif of a woman behind a high counter.

The waif looked up from her computer screen, pushing thick blond hair out of her eyes. "Welcome to ShapeShifters," she said. Her name was Susan, according to her name tag. She had one of those friendly but fierce faces that made Angela feel at home.

Angela placed her elbows on the counter and announced, "I'm here to lose five pounds."

"If I could get you to fill out this form first." Susan pushed a clipboard over the counter. "We can get you on that scale and start your weight-loss journey." Susan winked mechanically and gestured to a room full of chairs facing a whiteboard wall. Cheerfully written slogans like "The journey of a thousand miles begins with just one step" and "No cookie tastes better than skinny feels" radiated from the whiteboard and surrounding posters.

Angela hesitated, fighting an intense urge to flee. "How long will it take to lose five pounds?" she asked.

Susan stood on her tiptoes to survey Angela over the counter and scrunched up her little button nose. "Not sure you have five to lose," she said. "There's a pamphlet under your registration form there that will answer some preliminary questions. The rest we can discuss after."

Susan flashed a smile over Angela's shoulder. Next in line was a shiny-faced woman still panting, presumably from the stairs. The lobby had quietly filled with women waiting to be weighed.

"Thank you," Angela whispered, picking up the clipboard and making her way to a chartreuse chair near the meeting room's window.

A pleasant clatter of voices emanated from the lobby, all feminine in tone.

"Did you lose, Jo?"

"Two pounds."

"Wow! Way to go!"

"What did you do differently this time?"

"It hasn't been a banner week for me. Let's get it over with."

"I tried Zumba …"

"Brother's wedding …"

"Did you change your hair? You look great."

"Ugh. I almost didn't come today."

"That's when you know you really need the meeting."

"Happens to me every time I have pizza."

"It's the salt, I think."

"Chocolate is my weakness. French fries don't tempt me."

As Angela filled out the last box on her form, a male voice broke through the clatter. "My wife is needing help with fat," he said. There was a hush in the room as Angela turned to see who was speaking.

"Welcome to ShapeShifters," Susan said to the woman in front of her, ignoring the man. "If you could fill out this form and bring it back, we can get started on your weight-loss journey." The woman remained still behind a curtain of fabric. Angela could not see her eyes but imagined them cast downward as the man spoke for her again.

"I will write for her," he said, grabbing the clipboard off the counter and leading his shapeless companion to a row of chairs, pomegranate pink, near the lobby.

Only on television had Angela seen women covered in cloth everywhere but their eyes. Intrigue pulled her in like a magnet. *I'm not in Fairview anymore*, she thought, pushing back a wave of shame over the xenophobia pulsing through her birth place. She watched the man navigate the registration form with his pen. He scratched his beard and murmured questions to his wife, who sat motionless beside him, her pale blue gown pooling on the carpet over her feet. *What would lead a woman to believe her life is better faceless?* Angela wondered.

chapter 3

OF ALL THE SCENARIOS ANGELA HAD FRETTED OVER, BEING REJECTED WASN'T ONE OF THEM.

"We have a policy, you see," Susan explained after jotting down Angela's weight in a pink and green folder. "To join, you need to be at least five pounds over your optimal BMI weight."

"I don't understand," Angela said. "I have always weighed 155 at most, usually less. I'm at 161 now and"—she looked behind her to ensure no one was listening—"none of my usual tricks seem to be working."

Susan pointed to the number she just wrote, then to a chart on the wall. "You see, you are at a healthy weight now—"

"And I wasn't before, when I weighed 150 and felt great in my clothes?" Angela interrupted.

Susan placed her pointing hand on top of her head and squeezed her hair into a fist. "It's just that this program is meant to help those who are dangerously overweight—"

"Let me get this straight. You would have me go home, continue on with my life until I become dangerously overweight, at which point I would then, *only then*, be welcomed with open arms into your secret society of weight-loss tricks?"

"Strategies," Susan corrected.

"What?"

"We discuss weight-loss strategies, not tricks."

Angela blinked.

A few seconds passed before Susan attempted a sincere smile, signaling an end to the matter.

Angela employed her stand-there-without-speaking tactic. Eventually, Susan would have to fill the silence with something helpful. A concession, perhaps. She waited for Susan to wither from her intense stare and offer something constructive to end the stand-off.

Surprisingly unfazed, Susan looked at her watch and said, "I have to start the meeting now. Sorry I can't help. It's a rule, you see."

Defeated, Angela scooped up her purse from the chair by the scale and turned to leave. She paused and turned back. "Wait," she said. "Weigh me again, please."

"I really have to start the meeting."

"I think your scale was wrong. Let me have another go on that one." She pointed behind Susan to another scale in front of an unmanned weigh station.

Susan let out an exasperated sigh and marched over to the alternate scale. She bent over to plug it in beneath a table stacked with brochures. Then she pressed the "on" button and waited for the ready signal. After a few seconds, she stepped back so Angela could step on.

"There you have it," Angela said after the numbers settled on 163. "See you in the meeting then."

As Angela turned around to take a seat in the meeting room, Susan saw a phone and a coin purse bulging out of Angela's back pockets.

chapter

4

MINA HAVER WAS FOLLOWING A STREAM OF WOMEN LEAVING THE BUILDING WHEN HER HUSBAND POPPED OFF A BENCH WHERE HE'D BEEN WAITING.

"They gave me a job," Kushan said. He held up a brown paper bag. "I bought shawarma to celebrate."

What a relief, Mina thought. He had applied for many jobs since they arrived in Canada. Their sponsors had referred him for janitor, fast food server, and parking attendant positions, but Kushan was a proud man. Cutting hair was all he had known back in Qattinah. She wondered if he had sabotaged the interviews in the hopes of finding a hair-related job. "That is so good to hear," Mina said. "At the place here in the mall?"

"Yes!" Kushan smiled widely. "I offered to do anything there, even sweeping, making coffee, laundry. But the owner was running behind on her clients and one stylist had called in sick. She let me do a shampoo and trim on an impatient man." Kushan took Mina's arm and began walking toward the car. "The man was pleased and the owner hired me on the spot."

"Oh, Kushan. Shouldn't you have stayed?" Mina stopped to assess his expression. "If they are behind, she might need you all day."

"I offered," Kushan said, gesturing across the lot to their car. "She had arranged coverage the rest of the day." He winked at Mina and added, "I suspect a stylist might be fired."

Mina nodded, breathing in the spicy scent of the lamb sandwiches. "That smells good. Thank you."

"What did you learn in the weightless meeting?" Kushan asked once they were in the car, heading to the home their sponsors rented for them.

Mina thought about the main point of the presentation. There had been a back-and-forth dialogue between the leader and the members. Susan had drawn a series of emoji faces on the whiteboard to illustrate the skill for the week. "Being happy or sad can cause overeating. And it is weight loss, not weightless," she said.

"What?" Kushan looked at her skeptically, taking his

eyes off the road for a moment. Mina saw the accident before it happened, waving her hand frantically toward the windshield. Kushan stomped on the brake too late. They felt a soft thump before a woman crossing the street slipped from view.

Mina got out of the car immediately. Kushan followed moments later.

The woman, frail and wrinkled, was pulling herself up, both hands on the front bumper for support. "What the fridge?" she said, leveling her steely eyes at Kushan. "Are you blind to stop signs? Pedestrians have the right of way in this country." With one hand still on the bumper, she felt around the pavement underneath. Mina saw the cane, pulled it out from under the car, and handed it to her.

Kushan said, "I am sorry."

"You're sorry," the woman scolded. "You're sorry. I should report you. I have bad knees. Do you understand me?" She paused for Kushan's response. He looked around him, apparently stunned. Some other cars had stopped and more were beginning to drive around the altercation. A man in one of the cars, a white van, rolled down the window and asked if he could help. "I should report you," the woman said again. "I bet you don't even have a license."

Mina looked at her husband anxiously, silently pleading for him to say something other than sorry.

"I'm sorry," Kushan said again. Mina put her hands on her hips, willing him to say something, *anything* besides sorry. "Can I help?" This time he merely parrotted words from the man in the van.

The woman stared at him furiously, then turned her gaze to Mina. "I am only just beginning to recover from knee surgery. This will set me back," she said.

Mina did not know what to say. She began to worry all their hard work getting out of Syria would unravel if this woman complained to someone of importance. "Can we take you to a doctor?" she blurted, thinking how her own doctor explained her health predicament to Kushan. The doctor had placed her hands on Mina's hips and belly, then on her own slim frame to illustrate.

Redness drained from the woman's face as she took in Mina's burqa.

Mina felt a drop of sweat run down the back of her neck. She shrunk from the fierce eyes of this small woman, feeling vulnerable, naked. She had to look down at the pavement to interrupt the woman's glare.

"Do you need help?" the man in the van repeated. "Are you okay, ma'am?"

The woman waved at the man to continue on his way and turned her gaze back to Kushan. "I will not report you on one condition," she said. She glanced at Mina, who looked quickly to the pavement once more. "Send your wife to visit me once each week."

Kushan looked confused but Mina understood. "I can remove this offense by serving in her home each week," she explained.

chapter

5

ANGELA WAS STILL TRYING TO PUT TOGETHER HOW EMOTIONAL EATING MIGHT APPLY TO HER. Her neighborhood pub was alive with hockey fans when she met Mel after his day of meetings. She searched the menu for a grilled chicken salad and decided nachos with chicken was close enough. "Is joy a feeling?" Angela flicked a sprig of cilantro off her nacho chip.

"Of course it is. Why?" Melvin asked, just as the pro-Senators crowd in the pub whooped behind him. He looked up at the closest TV and watched the replay.

"I went to that weight-loss place today. The topic was

eating our feelings." Angela faked a smile, plunging her chip into a mound of guacamole.

"Oh, but honey," Melvin said, with mock schmaltz, "you look greeaaat."

Angela threw a naked chip at him. "Seriously! I am so joyful to be in this country, I celebrate non-stop." Chewing slowly, she noted a perfect ratio of goo to crunch. "Usually with food." She took a big swig of her Guinness. "And drink!"

Melvin eyed her over the top of his glass, swallowing the hoppy craft beer as slowly as he could for extra thinking time. "You're saying you've gained weight," he said, treading carefully.

"Look at this," she said, pinching her stomach.

Melvin winced, but caught himself before she noticed. "That's new?" he asked as cheerfully as possible. He let his eyes drift over her shoulder ever-so-slightly to see what was happening with the game.

Angela scowled, pushing her plate away. "Oh, forget I even brought it up."

Mel's strong, dark brow-line unfurled. "Game's over. Let's go get gelato." He plunked down some brightly colored bills.

Her plight forgotten just like that. Angela couldn't believe he took her words literally. Just once, she'd love an empathetic response from her matter-of-fact husband. The thought enveloped her in a cloud of loneliness. But the sight of Canadian money perked her back up. No need for empathy in a country where citizens' basic needs were met.

Then the waitress drifted past, wearing a black mini

skirt and snug V-neck. There were no folds of fat as she bent to clear their dishes. The nachos sat like lead in Angela's stomach, and the skin on her waist was so appalled, it crowded against her belt in fright.

Angela slipped on her jean jacket and headed for the doors. "No gelato for me. I'm going home."

On the other side of those doors was a wonderland of delights: trendy, candle-lit bars filled with pretty people sipping martinis; the pierogies place under the bookstore that transformed into a nightclub after 10:00 p.m.; and the old-style movie theater that breathed out buttered popcorn when you walked by. She and Mel had only begun to explore their new surroundings. The thought of curtailing their explorations to lose a couple of pounds depressed her.

"Oh, come on. Don't be boring." Melvin caught up to her as she made a beeline for home.

She stopped short. "Boring? That's not very helpful." She batted at a stray lock of hair blowing across her face. "I can't be fun all the time, can I? At some point, I have to find a purpose here. I mean other than escaping you-know-who."

Melvin sighed, took her hand, and turned in the direction of the river instead of downtown. "You have Jeremy. And me. We aren't enough of a purpose?"

They passed several houses. She loved the variety of each home. Newer structures stood sandwiched between 1940s-style farmhouses; they complemented each other in contrasting styles.

"You're the one who said you couldn't take another year of the Trump admin—"

Angela jerked her hand from his. "Don't say his name," she said, giving Mel a don't-test-me look.

"Sorry." Melvin slipped his hand back over hers. "You said you were ready to leave law and spend more time with us," he reminded her.

"I know. And I do want that still. I just …" How to put her restlessness into words? "I kind of thrived on the stress and responsibility."

"You miss the stress?"

"Well …" She tried to find the words for being full but not with food. "Yes. Yes, I do." There, she said it. "If I'm a stress addict, sue me."

Melvin laughed. He held one hand up in mock surrender.

"Maybe I *am* a stress addict. Is that a thing?"

They stopped in front of their house by the river. While Angela watched a twig do a slow dance in the river's current, Melvin took out his phone. "Nope." He showed her the results of his google search. "Not a thing."

Shadowy figures with leashed dogs meandered along the river bank. The water reflected a silvery moon. Angela felt her breathing slow and her spirits lift. Not one of those people would be carrying a gun. Would the peaceful feeling of this place ever get old? She hoped not.

chapter 6

SUSAN WAS NOT IN THE HABIT OF JUDGING THOSE IN HER WEIGHT-LOSS CARE. Empathy and community-building were, after all, essential tenets of shepherding a person through the drudgery of pound-shedding. Therefore, as she performed her store-opening rituals, she asked herself why she dreaded Angela's appearance.

The truth was, Angela got under her skin. No one had given her such trouble over a ShapeShifters rule before. When Angela asked to be weighed at another scale, Susan agreed for two reasons: to appease Angela so she could more firmly usher her back out the door, and to check one of the scales in the office because it had a tendency to produce inconsistent results. She was sure she had relegated that one to the cramped storage cubicle in the back. But if by remote chance she had stored a functioning one rather than the broken one, she didn't want other members (who had formed a longer-than-usual line behind Angela) to suffer after being made to wait. Her record of efficiently processing each member in two minutes was in jeopardy as long as Angela continued to stand her ground.

So when Angela stepped up for her weigh-in the next week, Susan's insides boiled. No matter how hard she tried to smile with warmth and concern, the corners of her mouth turned downward.

"You lost one pound," came out robotically. Then sarcasm hijacked her brain. "Did you lose a cell phone or a coin purse?" She winced and mentally chastised herself. She was supposed to say something helpful or constructive like, "What did you do differently this week?" But to her relief, no one else heard. And Angela did not call her on her rudeness.

"Ha ha," Angela replied without real amusement. She didn't look as stung as Susan had expected. Instead of recoiling, she turned around and lifted up her sweater. Like last week, the phone and change purse bulged from her back pockets. "Have to keep it real," she said a bit too cheerfully.

Susan focused on her computer screen, updating Angela's record. She peeled off a happy-face sticker from her stash of motivator tools and placed it on Angela's hand, giving her a smile she wished was more authentic. She had lost a pound, which required acknowledgment and a question to prompt the member to self-analyze. Susan took a deep breath and tried to force some enthusiasm into her voice. "Congrats. Not bad for your first week. Did you do anything differently?"

"Matter of fact, I skipped after-dinner drinks," Angela said, her blue eyes bright with pride. "Twice." She looked down toward her bleach white sneakers sheepishly. Susan waited a beat, conscious that further conversation would steal time from others. Angela gathered her purse and jean jacket. "I was trying to notice my emotions more. You know, like you said in the meeting last week. And I concluded that I might possibly joyful-eat, if there is such a thing."

Susan couldn't help but look at the line lengthening behind Angela. Her empathetic side glared harshly at her judgmental side. Angela was offering an opportunity to connect. Ordinarily, this would give Susan valuable insights that would foster a trusting relationship. But she wanted Angela to move on so she could help the next member with an actual weight-loss challenge.

"Oh, sorry," Angela said. She tapped her smiley-face sticker. "I'll let your more worthy members have you now." She rushed off to the meeting room before Susan could respond, leaving her to stew in her own shame.

As Angela stood at the back of the room, she saw the veiled woman from last week sitting in the second row of chairs. *A bit too close to the leader,* Angela thought, *but what the heck.*

The conundrum of this woman had plagued Angela all week. Images of faceless women had infiltrated her dreams. She had stared so long at a woman in the grocery who used scarves to cover her hair, ears, and neck, that the woman eventually backed her cart out and into another line to avoid Angela's gaze. And when Angela's head got stuck in the wide sleeve of a sweater she pulled on one morning and she found herself peering out of an arm-hole instead of the neck, she had lingered there for a few moments, peering into the mirror with her one visible eyeball. At first she felt cozy and safe, all covered up, with no need to assess her unwaxed eyebrows or uneven skin tone. But then the heat started to build, prompting her to shrug off the whole sweater in a fit of claustrophobia.

"Do you mind if I sit here?" Angela asked the woman. She couldn't see an expression behind the rectangular screen near the top of her head. But the woman's gaze landed on Angela abruptly, as if startled. Then a hand unfolded from a long, loose sleeve and patted the chair in question.

"My name is Mina," she said after Angela sat down.

"Oh! Very nice to meet you, Mina," Angela enthused. "I'm new to Canada, by the way. An American refugee, you might say, forced to seek sensible government, free from you-know-who." She tried to make her voice comically conspiratorial. Mina didn't laugh. Angela cleared her throat and added, "Have you lived here all your life?"

"No," Mina said. "We were privately sponsored after we ..." When Mina paused, Angela thought she heard a sniff. Mina brought a hand to her shrouded face and continued. "After we left our home in Syria."

"Oh my God, you're an actual refugee," Angela exclaimed too loudly. A trio of women in the front row turned to look at her, then went back to their conversation. "I'm sorry," Angela whispered. "I shouldn't have joked about being an American refugee. Running from a president I don't like is a first world luxury. Not that you're third world, I mean not anymore …" As Angela dug herself a deeper hole, she noticed Mina kept her head pointing forward. No reaction. This was Angela's chance to get to know someone unlike anyone she'd ever met, and she was blowing it. "Anyway, I'd love to hear your story sometime," she finally concluded, silently praying for the floor to open up and swallow her.

Just then, Susan came bounding into the room with a bluetooth speaker blaring the "I Like to Move It" song. She rocked out alone for a few seconds at the front of the room. "Doesn't this song make you want to get up and dance?" she asked the group. A few ladies nodded indulgently, some looked confused, and one lady in front moved her shoulder to the beat ever so slightly. Susan fiddled with her phone to turn off the music. "Alright then. After you hear how important movement is, you are going to be dancing with me by the end of this meeting."

Mina tilted her head to Angela and whispered, "I want to hear your story, too."

Angela's insides unraveled into a warm puddle of relief. She smiled at her companion, then allowed herself to give Susan her full attention.

"Research shows that twenty minutes a day is all we need for exercise," Susan was saying. "And we can spread those twenty minutes out. Five minutes here climbing stairs, ten minutes there walking to lunch, ten minutes walking the dog … and so on." She strolled around the room and smiled meaningfully at the members, imitating each action she described. "What else can you do with twenty minutes?"

"Walk to the grocery," a pleasantly plump senior with purplish hair volunteered.

"Good one." Susan nodded appreciatively. "What else?"

Other people started chiming in.

"I can walk the perimeter of our neighborhood in twenty minutes," one said.

"I squeeze my bum at the lights when I'm driving," said another. Mild giggles at this.

"Sex!" said a buxom blond in the back. Laughter at that.

Susan pressed something into the hand of each person who contributed to the discussion. "You don't have to run a marathon or climb Everest. Just get up off your chair as much as you can and move," she said as she walked and pressed.

Angela's hand shot up and Susan nodded. (Did she hesitate slightly?) "Does it hurt to run a marathon?" Angela asked. She and Melvin had brainstormed some purposeful goals, and starting a running program appealed the most to her. Previous attempts to run had lasted ten minutes or less, but she'd always wanted to get through that wall.

Susan looked down at her notes for a few seconds. "I can't vouch for the safety of any particular exercise program," she said. "That would be between you and your doctor." She placed a sticker in Angela's hand—a thumbs-up symbol.

"The idea today is to emphasize that small steps are the best way to tackle movement," Susan said to the group.

"Some of us have to fight our perfectionist notions that get in the way of healthy activity."

She raised her own hand and added, "Anyone else here a perfectionist? Ever say to yourself you can't go to the gym today because you only have thirty minutes instead of an hour?"

Two or three hands went up.

Susan nodded in a guilty-as-charged kind of way. "Once," she said, "I drove all the way to the gym." She raised an eyebrow. "And when I couldn't get my usual treadmill, I turned around and drove home."

Angela looked around the room and saw mostly shocked and amused faces. She couldn't relate to that one, but a tiny part of her liked Susan more.

"True story," Susan said. "The next time, I set a very modest goal: to try a new machine for five minutes." Susan smiled at the chatter and giggles that followed. "Who wants to tell me their doable exercise goal for next week?"

She let at least ten seconds go by, and finally someone said, "Maybe I'll take the bus to work this week instead of drive." Susan grinned and dispatched a sticker.

More goals and sticker handouts followed as Angela struggled with the question. Training for a marathon seemed too big all the sudden. She would have to rethink her exercise goals.

"Before I forget," Susan said. "The ShapeShifters annual 7k run is coming up. See me after the meeting for more information if you're interested."

Bingo.

"So," Angela said to Mina as she stood up and fished her purse from under her perky pink chair, "Did you have a good week, weight-loss wise?"

"No," Mina said. "I gained weight."

Angela searched the screen in Mina's veil, conjuring a pair of mahogany eyes peering dolefully from its depths.

"How did it go for you?" Mina asked.

"I lost a pound," Angela said guiltily. "Had to cut back on my celebratory eating and drinking." She still wasn't sure if joyful eating was a credible cause for weight gain.

"Celebratory?" Mina asked. "Like a holiday?"

"No, no," Angela laughed. "I seem to have more time on my hands since I left the States. And we are so excited to be here." She wondered how inane this must seem to Mina, assuming she understood it at all. "We just celebrate all the time." She felt awkward and pitiful before the blankness of Mina's unmoving head. "We go from restaurant to bar to club to diner ... we eat out a lot," she clarified, willing herself to shut up. "Anyway." She was desperate to change the subject. "I'm going to ask Susan about the 7k. Hard to eat and drink when you're running, right? Hey! Maybe we could sign up together?" She blurted this out before she could think it through. Looking down at Mina's long gown, noticing how it completely covered her shoes, Angela fought an intense urge to flee. To her horror, she kept talking. "If um ... is running something you can do?" she asked lamely.

Mina stood up and slipped her hand under Angela's elbow. "I don't know," she said. "Let's go find out."

chapter 7

MINA STEPPED OFF THE BUS AND PULLED HER SHAWL TIGHTLY AROUND HER SHOULDERS. The shawl was a gift from their sponsors at Mount Pleasant United.

One of the church volunteers, a kindly woman wearing a tight turtleneck and sweatpants, had shown up the first crisp fall day. She had taken Mina to a dental appointment and resisted her invitation to stay for dinner. The frazzled woman had plunked down a grocery bag of fresh zucchini along with the shawl before rushing away.

Mina had no recipes for zucchini, but she appreciated

the shawl. It was made of something unnaturally soft and warm.

Her jaw still ached. She tried not to run her tongue over the two gaping holes in her mouth like the dentist said. But she seemed to remember only after her tongue had landed there.

But Mina felt more stung by Laila's attitude. She had walked Laila partway to school that morning. Laila stopped abruptly before they reached the bus stop. "They'll make fun of me," she'd said. "Parents don't walk teenagers to school." Perhaps Canada was a safer country than Syria, but the way Laila said it made Mina feel useless. And angry.

Earlier she had packed a lunch of lamb and eggplant stew with *manoushi* bread for Kushan and kissed him goodbye. He would be gone all day and most of the evening. He had been promoted twice after mentioning his ability to duplicate celebrity hair styles. Mina didn't recognize the celebrity names he mentioned, but his clients were impressed by this art of matching a celebrity with their face and turning the clients into movie stars before their very eyes. He was in such a good mood, he had been pestering her for love-making twice a day. She smiled despite her jaw. They were like teenagers again. When she handed him his lunch, he had a twinkle in his eyes. Then Laila came out of the shower and saw them embracing. She rolled her eyes, prompting Kushan to leave for work laughing.

As she rode the bus, Mina thought about Laila's rudeness and Kushan's voiceless acceptance of lunch. And she ignored the odd sensation of people's eyes boring into the back of her head. No one attempted to speak to her on the bus. They pretended she wasn't there.

Mina double-checked the old woman's address. It was not far from the strip mall where Mina got her groceries. She hoped to stop there after her visit to buy lentils for cooking with chicken and spinach for dinner.

She followed the sidewalk through a park. There were tennis courts dusted with frost. A public hockey space was being built between the tennis courts and a school. She took in the school's basketball hoop and play structure standing unappreciated on a bed of wood chips. She wondered whether Laila had opportunities to exercise outside. There would be no gunfire or explosions to punctuate her school day.

Mina ambled along a driveway that wove through a cluster of small houses pressed so tightly together they reminded her of a boat packed with too many people. The old woman's house was on the far corner. Her doorstep had a bristly mat, its red poppy design faded and dingy. The door, with peeling blue paint, opened before she could press the doorbell.

The woman stood before Mina wearing stretchy black pants and gray knit slippers. Her sweater, beige with a stripe of red and another of charcoal, was buttoned up over a yellow turtleneck dotted with tiny blue flowers. Her smile, welcoming and warm at first, vanished quickly behind a scowl.

"Well come in, then. You're letting all the hot air out. Jesus." She stepped behind the door to let Mina through, then pushed it shut with a shiver. "You can leave your shoes there." She pointed to an ankle-level rack along the wall by the door.

Mina looked around for signs of men in the house. The door opened into a kitchen opposite a darkened hallway beyond a round table with two chairs. There were brown cupboards along a speckled white countertop on one side of the kitchen. A square needlepoint clock on a powder blue wall on the other side had a quivering hand ticking along a flowered canvas. Mina smelled coffee and saw some percolating on the counter by the sink. Other than the tick of the clock and gurgle of the coffee pot, she heard no sounds. "Do you live alone?" she asked the woman.

The woman fixed her steely eyes on Mina. "Kind of a personal question, isn't it?"

Mina aimed her chin toward the dark hallway.

"Oh, for Pete's sake," the woman huffed. "No one's going to bother us. Are you staying or going?"

Mina slipped off her white Skechers, careful not to show the soles of her socks, and placed them next to a pair of brown boots.

"Coffee?" The woman was already filling two cups. "I don't have tea."

"Thank you," Mina said. The kitchen was invitingly warm.

"Well, have a seat." She gestured to the chair closest to Mina.

A cane leaned against the counter near the sink. "Can I help you?" Mina asked. She was not accustomed to being served by elders.

"Sit," the woman said, ignoring her question. She stepped gingerly over to the table with the cups gently rattling against their saucers and set them down. Then she placed both hands on her end of the table to ease herself into a chair. "You can call me Kelly."

"It's a pleasure to meet you, Mrs. Kelly. My name is Mina."

"Mina," Kelly said as if eating something too chewy. "What kind of name is that?"

Mina pondered the question. "It's my name."

Kelly took a sip of her coffee, keeping her eyes on Mina. Mina had the impression she was waiting for her to make a mistake or be caught in a lie. The clock ticked along. Mina lifted her niqab enough to drink, sipping the bitter liquid quickly and returning the dainty cup to its saucer on the table. When she set it down, the soft clink was louder than it should be.

"I have to be honest with you, Mina," Kelly finally said. "It's harder than I thought talking to someone I can't see. Are you smiling or frowning? Are you nervous or relaxed? It's rather distracting."

Mina smiled for the first time, emboldened by the woman's honesty. "I'm smiling," she said.

Kelly nodded and looked up at the clock. "Well, I suppose you have things to do."

"I'm here to serve you," Mina said. "To repay your kindness. Thank you for forgiving my husband. How is your knee?"

The woman waved her hand like she was repelling an

irritating insect. "Oh, don't be a ninny. I've been through worse. Do you play any games?"

Mina remembered the basketball hoop and the half-constructed hockey rink. "I never learned."

"I like war," Kelly said.

Mina recoiled and her heart raced. Images of headless bodies and topless buildings flew through her mind. Panting, her hands clinging to the edge of the table, she managed to say between breaths, "War is no game."

Kelly sat back in alarm, her body rigid. "Not a … oooh." Letting out a "hoo hah" kind of laugh, she pushed herself up out of her chair with both hands and shuffled over to a drawer. Taking out a rectangular box, white with repetitive red dots, she held it up so Mina could see. "It's a card game."

Mina watched Kelly totter back to the table, open up one end of the box, and shake out the contents. Stiff rectangular papers with a design on one side and numbers on the other spilled out across the table. The non-threatening manner in which Kelly spoke and acted brought Mina back to herself. She stopped panting. Her heart behaved itself.

"Do you know cards?" Kelly waved her hand over the mess on her table and softened her voice.

Mina looked at the cards, then at Kelly. "This is war?"

"Cards." Kelly tapped one of them. "They're called cards. You can play games with them. To pass the time. Can I teach you?"

Mina nodded once. She peeled her sweaty palms from the table and pushed back her shoulders in relief.

Kelly shuffled the cards. After that, she slid the whole

deck over to Mina. "Now you split the deck however you like and put the top on the bottom." She made a show of how it was done without actually doing it.

Mina accepted the cards and picked up only a few from the top, stacked them to the side, then took the rest of the pile and stacked them on top of the few.

Kelly looked impressed, raising an eyebrow while pulling the stack back to her side of the table. Next, she peeled one card off the top and placed it decorative side up on Mina's side of the table. Mina started to pick it up to see what she'd won, but Kelly put her hand on Mina's. "Wait. Not yet," she said.

She peeled off another card and put it decorative side up on her end of the table. She looked at Mina with raised eyebrows that clearly conveyed, "Wait" again, then peeled off another card and put it on top of Mina's first card. After that, the setup happened quickly, one card on Kelly's pile, the next on Mina's, another card on Kelly's, the next on Mina's, and so on until there were no more cards left in the original stack.

"Okay," Kelly said, with a gleam in her eye. "Now we begin." Kelly took her half-pile and smoothed out the edges into a neat stack. Mina did the same. Then the woman peeled off the first card in the stack and placed it in the middle of the table, non-decorative side up. There was just one shape in the middle, red in color. The woman nodded at Mina's stack. Mina peeled off the top card and put it next to the woman's, non-decorative side up. Mina's card was filled up with designs that looked like three black dots blooming from a single black stem. "I win," Kelly said, scooping up both cards and placing them below the pile of cards on her side of the table.

"I have more decorations," Mina said.

Kelly's mouth fell open, bringing her eyebrows down. Mina tried to think what she'd done wrong. Then Kelly grinned. "Ace is highest," she said. She turned over her ace again and pointed to the diamond in the middle. "One is the best," she said, showing Mina her index finger.

One bomb killing multiple people, leveling multiple buildings. Mina peeled off the next card and placed it in the center. It featured two heart shapes, red in color. She was pleased to get the love card, not war.

The woman peeled off a card and placed it next to the two hearts. It was filled with the blooming three dots shapes. Mina looked at Kelly for confirmation that multiple blooming flower shapes conquered two hearts. The woman nodded and dragged the two cards to her side of the table.

The game continued, with Mina learning eventually that shapes were less important than how many times they repeated. When the original pile of cards was doled out, Mina had a smaller pile than Kelly's. Kelly seemed less intense now, the lids over her eyes revealing more of themselves. Mina looked at the clock. Her window for gathering food and preparing it was closing. But she couldn't disappoint Kelly.

The woman pressed herself up from the table and said, "You catch on quickly, Mina." She picked up the empty coffee cups and walked them gingerly over to the sink. "I don't want to keep you from your family duties," she said with a hint of melancholy.

"I lost the war?" Mina asked.

Kelly smiled meekly. "This time. Next time, who knows?"

A smaller pile equaled loss. Mina jumped up to wash the dishes in the sink. Kelly appeared too tired to object, grabbing her cane for the first time, finding her way back to her chair, and slumping into it. Mina finished up the dishes and saw the fatigue in Kelly's posture. She took Kelly by the elbow and helped her up. "Where can you rest?"

The woman pointed to the door through the hallway and, together, they traveled to a moss green couch one room away. Kelly was asleep as soon as her head hit the throw-pillow, breathing deeply and peacefully. Mina took a crocheted blanket from the back of a chair and draped it over Kelly. She watched her for a few ticks of the needlepoint clock to make sure she was indeed at peace, then made her way back to the kitchen. The small table at which they sat moments before seemed intolerably bare without coffee cups and cards. She glanced at the clock and quickly slipped out the door.

chapter

8

SUSAN MADE SCONES FOR LEX AND ESTER EVERY MORNING AT SIX O'CLOCK. Blueberry was the favorite. She had perfected the moist-insides-crispy-outsides texture they loved. When the other kids were around, she'd make date with oats for Kimberly and plain for Caleb. He liked his with strawberry jam.

But before scones, she'd start a pot of coffee and stand by the patio doors looking for rabbits. Today was gray and cold. No sign of bunnies. As she set the coffee pot back on the burner, she nearly collided with Ester.

"God, Mom. You can't just walk around with a pot of

coffee. Geez, you almost burned me." Ester dropped her gym bag in the middle of the floor between the island and the counter where Susan headed with the coffee pot. She scanned the island quickly. "No scones today?"

"It never occurred to me I'd run into my teenage daughter anywhere outside of her bedroom at five in the morning," Susan said, wiping a few drops of coffee from the counter. "I was just about to make the scones." She turned around to find Ester's head buried in the fridge. "You okay?"

"I'd be better if I could find my green juice," Ester said from inside the fridge. "Ugh, here it is. Behind the banana bread Tupperwares." She withdrew from the fridge, holding a bottle of green liquid. The label proclaimed "Pro Max Blast" under a lightning bolt. Green fruits and vegetables spun out from the bolt. "How many different types of banana bread do we need?" Ester asked, slamming the fridge door.

"Well, you like the kind with chocolate chips and I can't handle the sugar and gluten, so …"

"And the other two?"

"Experiments. I'm working on a vegan version. What is that horrid-looking sludge you have there?"

Ester unscrewed the cap and guzzled it. She puckered, then let out a breathy, "Aaaahhhh … that's the stuff." After setting it down, she began rummaging through her gym bag.

Susan picked up the bottle and read the ingredients. "There are a lot of things in here I can't pronounce."

"So?" Ester extracted a hoody and slipped it on over her tank top.

"So the label looks like you're drinking liquified healthy things. But I don't see those things in the ingredient list."

"It's what people are drinking, Mom," she said, feigning annoyance. "Banana bread is out. Green detox juice is in. Try to keep up." Ester took the bottle from her mother and tossed it across the room into the trash bin. "She shoots, she scores!"

"There's no such thing as a detox anything." Susan walked over to the trash bin. "Your body does all the detoxing you need by itself." She extracted the bottle, shaking her head.

Ester rolled her eyes. "Can I go now?"

"All I'm saying is it's not that complicated." Susan set the glass in a recycling tub under the sink. "Just eat and drink real foods." She gave Ester a kiss on the cheek. "Throw some spinach and kiwi in a blender if you want to drink healthy green things. You don't need a bunch of chemicals with a misleading label."

"Funny." Ester headed out, slinging the clunky bag over her shoulder.

"What's funny?"

"You. Saying *it's not complicated* when you have five different banana breads in the fridge." Ester grabbed the car keys from a bowl in the hallway, gave her mom a sly smile, and bounced out the door.

"Well, at least I know what's in the banana bread!" Susan yelled at the closed door.

But now she was curious. Could she make a teenager-approved green smoothie? Eyeing the fruit bowl, she spotted one overripe banana. Five minutes later, she was sampling a blended concoction of banana, spinach, pear, lime, almond milk, and cashew butter from her Vitamix. Not bad.

Not good either. Making some notes on her phone, she tried some other combinations until she ran out of produce. Before making the scones, she recorded the parts that worked and the parts that didn't in a ShapeShifters Recipe file she created for members with unique food challenges. There was a recipe there for every need her members had expressed over the years.

If Ester was entranced by this detox drink phase, it would only be a matter of time before a member mentioned it. Susan labeled her work-in-progress "Me-Tox Green Juice." It shouldn't be that complicated, which gave her another idea. Before moving on to scones, she changed the file's name from "ShapeShifters Recipes" to "It's Not Complicated."

"Ha!" she said out loud. That would be a good name for a healthy cookbook.

chapter

9

ANGELA'S NERVES WERE AMPED AS SHE WALKED TO THE FIRST TRAINING RUN. They were to meet at the pedestrian bridge that crossed a pond brimming with geese. *Maybe that second cup of coffee was a bad idea,* she realized, her heart fluttering madly as her anxiety spiked. Would she quit before the run was over? What if she wore out her muscles walking there and got an injury? What if she was the slowest person in the group? What if she was the fastest and had to pretend she was slow? What if Susan copped an attitude and asked her not to participate because her un-obese presence might discourage the others? What if she got a cramp? What if she had to pee? *Oh God, now I have to pee …*

Something about the pond consoled her. As she approached the bridge, she took in the trees, on the verge of changing colors. Leaves tinged with green melded into brighter, warmer shades. Geese paddled around lazily, and the water reflected the gentle slope of the antique bridge and surrounding trees. The crisp air refreshed her. She could see a skiff of ice on parts of the pond.

She walked up the ramp to the bridge and saw Mina at the center chatting with Susan and the purple-haired lady. Mina wore the pale blue burqa. Angela wondered if they came in sportier versions. Purple Hair wore black yoga tights with a red and black hoodie stretched tightly over her bulging stomach and hips. To Angela's surprise, Susan waved cheerfully, beckoning her to join the little group.

"Angela, thanks for coming," Susan said. She was wearing skinny jeans and a bright pink puffy coat. *Strange running wear, but to each their own,* Susan thought. "I feel terrible about this," Susan continued, "but I have to pick up my daughter from ringette tryouts. I thought I'd get you to lead the group today."

Angela's urge to pee got stronger. "Um, I don't run. That's why I'm here."

A rather large woman with a ski jacket sauntered up to the group, engaging Mina and Purple Hair in conversation.

Susan put her arm around Angela and turned her slightly away from the group, lowering her voice. "I understand I'm putting you in an awkward position, and I'm sorry. But you are the fittest one here." She stated it like a fact. "And I really have no options other than canceling the first training run."

Canceling it? That would be disappointing. She walked all the way here, after all, and expended all that energy. Angela sighed. "What do I need to do?"

Susan smiled gratefully and handed her a paper with the workout plan. "It's the first session, so very manageable. Just make sure you do the warm-up exercises first and the stretching ones at the end. We don't want to injure anyone. I've already mentioned they should speak with their doctors, if they haven't already, to make sure they are fit to exercise. Today, it's just two kilometers. I've placed a little pink flag near the path at the turn-around point that way." She gestured toward the path on the other side of the bridge from where Angela walked. "It's just run for one minute, walk for two, over and over until you're back at the start. Then stretch, and off you go!" Susan looked at her watch. "I'm sorry. I'm late," she said, turning to rush off.

"Wait," Angela said. "What's ringette?"

Susan shot Angela a puzzled look. She seemed to mentally assess whether Angela was yanking her chain or not. "It's like hockey, but with rings," she finally said. After saying goodbye to the others, Susan jogged off the bridge, leaving Angela to lead the group.

"Hi, Mina," Angela said. "Got your running shoes?"

Mina looked nervously around. Then she lifted her gown with one hand to reveal the toe of a hot-pink striped running shoe.

"Wonderful! You're all set." She turned to the other two

and held out her hand. "I'm Angela and I'm not a runner." They laughed appreciatively.

"I'm Belinda. I used to run track but that was ages ago," said Purple Hair.

"Happy to meet you, Belinda. You know more than I do, then. Please share any and all wisdom you may have as we get going today." Belinda's cheeks turned a bit pink as she looked down at her black and white runners.

"I'm Joanne," said ski-jacket woman. "You can call me Jo. And I'm not a runner either." She glanced quickly at the others. "Am I overdressed?"

Belinda folded her arms as if to indicate it was indeed cold enough for a ski jacket. Angela said, "I think we're about to find out. Let's get warmed up first." She unfolded the paper Susan placed in her hands moments before. On it were cartoon-like people illustrating how the warm-up exercises went. "Right, so let's begin by jogging in place slowly while moving our arms in wide circles." She demonstrated and the group moved along with her, Belinda almost whacking Mina in the head.

"Perhaps we should spread out a little," Mina said.

"I'm so sorry," Belinda said, moving back a couple of feet from the circle and fanning her hands aggressively, like propellers on a plane.

After the warm-ups, Angela realized she had no watch and left her phone at home. Jo volunteered to call out the minutes, using her watch that also monitored her heart, counted her steps, and measured distance. As they started off their first minute, Angela noticed Belinda straining to take the lead, her arms pumping fast. "You go, girl!" Angela cheered.

Mina tripped a couple of times on the hem of her gown before sheepishly lifting up the front with one hand so she could run unobstructed. She held her other arm straight along her side. Her gait reminded Angela of a lady running to catch her flight in the airport the day she and Mel flew into Mount Pleasant.

Jo broke into a sweat immediately and unzipped her coat thirty seconds in, letting the zippered flaps whip about in the wind. She hovered a few seconds behind Angela and Mina, wheezing.

At the first walk break, the four of them came back together and caught their breath. "Well, that went well?" Angela said, looking around at each of them hopefully. Jo nodded but couldn't seem to speak and looked at her watch, presumably to check her heart rate.

Belinda was all smiles, her moist eyes bright with pride. "Much better than I thought," she said.

Mina just walked along quietly, her feet shuffling beneath her gown unencumbered, both arms straight at her sides. "You okay, Mina?" Angela asked.

"Yes, thank you. A bit warm though."

"Are you allowed to take off that thing?" Jo asked Mina. There was an awkward silence as the three of them held their collective breath, waiting for Mina to answer. A man wearing a University of Ottawa sweatshirt dashed past, his backpack swinging erratically behind him. Mina's head turned to survey his passing. Before she could answer, Jo's watch beeped. "Time to run!" Jo bellowed, and Belinda fanned her arms forward.

The rest of the session went uneventfully with little conversation. Back at the bridge, Angela took out Susan's paper and demonstrated some stretches, hitting as many of the leg muscles as she could. She was surprised at how tight her Achilles tendons were. Jo complained of a cramp in her calf.

They lined up along the side of the bridge to do the last stretch, each woman holding the rail with one hand and catching a foot from behind to stretch their quads. Jo couldn't reach her foot and inched closer to Mina. "Hey, I didn't mean to offend you back there," she said. "I was dying in my jacket and I … well, sorry if I misspoke."

"It's okay," Mina said. "It's my choice to wear this. I'm pleased I finished the run." Jo smiled, clapped Mina on her back, and reached around fruitlessly for her foot again.

chapter 10

SUSAN DROVE LIKE A BAT OUT OF HELL TO REACH THE ARENA IN A TIMELY MANNER. When she reached the parking lot, Ester wasn't outside yet. She parked the car and walked inside but saw no one in the skating rink. She peeked in the locker room, but there was no one there either. *Hmm*, she thought. *Am I at the wrong place?* She pulled out her phone and saw Ester had texted her. "Practice ended early. Heading to David's Tea with the girls. Melanie will drive me home." Susan fought the urge to throw her phone.

Ester had transformed into an entirely different human since she hit Grade 11. She had always been the model child, joining every athletic team there was; getting all A's; negotiating fiercely with the teachers who thought they were doing her a favor by handing out A-minuses despite completing projects and tests perfectly; aligning herself with throngs of adventurous friends; and becoming MVP of the cross-country ski, field hockey, and volleyball teams. She was still all those things, but suddenly her humble, helpful demeanor had morphed into a facade of overly-confident entitlement.

Usually, Susan could overlook it. Who was she to complain for having a daughter doing everything she'd been raised to do? No one got through the teenage years unscathed.

Her son Caleb was the worst, flouting curfews and contradicting her on every parental decision. Kimberly was a typical middle child, never causing trouble, always covering up for her siblings and smoothing things over before parenting could be done. But she was sneaky. She started dating before she was sixteen, despite her parents' clear rules. They didn't find out about it until she was well into her senior year. Caleb helped her get a fake ID so she could go to bars in Grade 9. Kimmy looked well beyond her years at that age. Neither Susan nor Lex caught on, and she had been drinking for four years by the time they celebrated her nineteenth birthday at the Mill Street Pub.

Ester, though. Her sudden nonchalant disregard for her parents' feelings and opinions was unexpected. Susan recalled the tears of joy in Ester's eyes when they adopted a puppy. Although Lex had pet allergies, he agreed to a dog when they saw how lonely Ester looked after Kimmy left for university.

When the puppy leaped out of the crate, adorned with a giant pink bow, into Ester's open arms, she dissolved into a puddle of tears. Even Lex choked up. They cautioned Ester that she was responsible for training the energetic little mutt and for exercising him.

Ester agreed instantly. She hugged her parents every morning, thanked them repeatedly, surprised them with their favorite coffees purchased with babysitting money, and filled the house with the maple aroma of pancakes on Saturdays before catching a ride to the ski hill or soccer game.

It never occurred to Susan that this grateful, humble, deserving young angel of theirs would so quickly dispense with these appreciative gestures. That she would allow the dog to go hours and hours without play time or walks to the point of their house being ransacked regularly by puppy benders. That she would slough off all threats of losing the dog as no big deal.

Lex and Susan decided to give the dog to a grateful neighbor who had volunteered to walk him (that's how much the neighbor loved him). Upon learning the dog was gone, Ester just shrugged her shoulders without comment on her way upstairs after school.

Susan was furious, reading Ester's glib text. When she punched in Ester's number on her phone, the call rolled to voice mail. Instead of leaving a message, Susan texted: "Abandoned my SS running group to pick you up. Saw your message AFTER reaching the arena. UNCOOL." Before tapping send, she searched for the red-faced angry emoji and added it to the end. Then she selected the angry emoji again and re-sent it so the face would be bigger the second time.

Susan looked at her watch. The training run would be over by now, so she headed home. When she unlocked her front door, she was greeted by a house so empty the silence felt stifling. She briefly considered getting a dog of her own, perhaps a calmer adult rescue, so she could have an appreciative little face to greet her. Then she remembered all the walking and poop-scooping and vet visits and searching for care when they traveled. She peeled off her fleece and flung it at the hall closet.

Maybe today will be the day I perfect my gluten-free almond scone recipe, she consoled herself, heading to the kitchen. Recipe experiments always soothed her.

chapter 11

MINA WAS WILLING TO DO ANYTHING TO HELP HER DAUGHTER SUCCEED IN HER NEW SCHOOL. But learning French?

On the bus ride home from her run, Mina sat staring at an advertisement. "$5 French Conversation Practice," it said. She and Kushan had mastered English before they arrived in Canada, but they had not counted on French being a required part of the curriculum in Mount Pleasant. Mina memorized the contact information, imagining Laila's surprise to have her mother's assistance on French homework.

When she got off the bus, she was shocked at how stiff

she was. She stretched her legs for a few minutes like Angela had taught them. Her stiffness subsided as she walked, and hunger swelled up in her stomach.

Inside the door, she removed her burqa and took off her runners. Her lycra tights and dry-fit shirt were damp and cold against her skin. She planned to have an apple for lunch, but as she prepared some rice and potatoes for dinner, her stomach growled. She took some bites from the apple while the food simmered and inspected the fridge for something small but filling to take the edge off.

No one in the ShapeShifters meeting was familiar with her style of cooking, but she heard a few of them who had good results with their weight talking about a certain type of yogurt that got them through the tough spots. She spotted the yogurt at the grocery but was disappointed to see its price. She would blow her food budget if she bought the yogurt for herself. She bought tunafish instead. Reaching for the tin in the cabinet above the stove, she popped off the lid and tried a few bites. Not too bad. Filling. She ate the whole tin and finished her apple. Then she drained three glasses of water.

When the food was done, she turned off the burner, scooped up her burqa, and headed toward the bathroom to bathe. Glancing at the clock, she knew Laila would be home any minute. In the window by the door, she saw Laila a half-block away, stooping over her unzipped backpack on the sidewalk. Her daughter was wearing a low-cut T-shirt with "Plastic Kills" written on it. Amazed, Mina watched as Laila pulled out the items they had designed and sewn together—a pink and silver gown and headscarf—which Laila was now draping around her head and body. Laila tucked in a few locks of hair, smoothing out the wrinkles around her waist. Mina experienced something like shock and shame as she watched her daughter transform from a Western-style teenager back into the modestly covered child with whom she'd walked partway to the bus that morning. Before Laila got to the door, Mina hurried down the hall and started the bathtub water running.

The warm water eased the strain in her muscles, but the pain in her heart remained. She had found her running shoes at a thrift store. They felt like pillows beneath her feet. She congratulated herself on finishing her first training run, despite the obstacle of her dress. "I choose to dress this way," she had told Jo. It was touching that Jo asked, and that she cared enough to apologize after. Now her daughter was choosing not to dress that way. And to hide her choice. Mina struggled to assimilate these ideas. Fought the pain her daughter's secrecy created. Was Laila ashamed? Had someone less conscientious than Jo jolted Laila out of herself? Mina's chest burned with anger as she considered the cruelty of other humans. The ignorance.

Breathing deeply, Mina calmed herself with memories of her own childhood, sitting beside her mother as they sewed. Mina and her three sisters learned everything from their mother. There was no school. Just their mother and her mother's friends. From these women spilled out truths, skills, practiced patience that would guide their actions, steady their steps as they tottered toward the future.

And yet. Mina and Kushan strongly believed children should go to school. So passionate was their conviction, it became a driving force for securing their passage out of Syria.

The constant worry of what they would eat, when and where the next bomb would fall, and which of the men in their village would disappear—these things added to their passion to leave. But securing a better future for their children was what worked itself into a frenzy in their hearts.

Mina considered what they lost. A cloud of gloominess crept along her insides. She fought it off, as she always did, telling herself how much worse off they would be if they had not come to Canada. She imagined the atrocities that would have crossed their paths eventually and her thoughts rested on the most obvious: the loss of everything they had, the loss of everyone they loved, the loss of hope, and an abrupt end to all their lives.

Mina clutched a soapy loofah to her heart, casting about for a way to communicate with Laila. After all their hard work, after all their struggles, after the greatest grief Mina had ever experienced, how had she not anticipated her daughter shrugging off the fabric of her heritage between home and the school? When did the gulf open up between mother and daughter?

Mina rinsed her hair, pulled the drain, and toweled off. She brushed the tangles from her hip-length hair and braided it with deft fingers, piling the long braid into a coil along the nape of her neck. She slipped on a pair of floral print pants, snapped on a clean bra, and pulled on a black

V-neck sweater. She stared back at her reflection in the mirror, conscious of all the bumps and bulges along her body. The glossy sheen of her hair, the line of her cleavage, and the curve of her hips reassured her. When she left the bathroom, she had the courage to tread carefully. To work pointedly to find a bridge back to Laila.

"Laila," she called out. "How was your day?"

chapter

12

ANGELA FILLED SOME TIME DOING LAUNDRY BEFORE JEREMY CAME HOME FROM SCHOOL. Hearing the door slam, she called out, "Jeremy? That you?" The front door was two floors below, and Jeremy's room a floor below that. If he was already in his room, he wouldn't hear her.

She shoved her running clothes, along with a pile of delicates, into the washer. The long mirror at the end of the narrow hallway between her bedroom and the office reflected a rosy-cheeked woman refreshed from her outdoor endeavors. In her sleeveless ruffled blouse, the offending bulge of her stomach was hidden, and she was content. She took a moment to be present. She had set out to train for something and she accomplished step one. Not only that, she led a few others without losing any of them along the way. *This is a good feeling*, she thought. And no martinis were sipped to obtain it.

She looked up at the next set of stairs that led to the rooftop patio. The roof was her favorite floor. It had a view of the downtown skyline on one side, the river on the other. True, the snow would eventually seal them inside, but three or four months of rooftop lounging would be worth the crazy amount of stairs required to access their oversized treehouse.

She descended the open-concept stairs to the kitchen level and heard Jeremy's steps on the flight below. They met near the piano, Jeremy looking a bit flushed. "Why do we have all these stairs?" he said.

Angela laughed and gave him a hug, which he barely returned. The little boy who used to hug her for no reason had become more man-like, more conscious of the woman than the mom in his stepmom. "Come on now, you love the roof," she said. "And having the basement to yourself." An image popped into her head. A memory of Jeremy jumping in a pile of leaves at age seven. He wore a fleece sweater she'd bought him that day. Unprompted, he ran over to her, gave her a giant bear hug, and said "Thanks for the sweater." He took her hand to show her how soft it was. "It feels like a hug!" In an instant he was back at the leaf pile, leaving Angela in a cloud of warmth.

Now he walked around her to the wall of flush white cabinets and pulled out a box of Vector cereal. "What I love," he said sarcastically, "is being the new guy at a high school so far from my friends I might as well be on Mars."

Angela chose to ignore this. "Don't ruin your appetite. We're doing steak and *frites* tonight."

He opened the fridge and grabbed the milk. "I definitely hate these weird milk bags." He poured some on his cereal, a few drops flying outside the bowl before the liquid settled into a pour.

Angela wet a dishcloth and handed it to him. "I'll give you that," she said. "Easier to walk home with a plastic jug of milk than a bulky bag of three smaller bags."

Jeremy sat at the table, crunching his cereal. He started a video on his phone and put in the ear buds hanging around his shoulders.

"Jeremy." Angela took one of the buds out of his ear and sat down next to him. "Can we talk?"

He set his spoon down. "Can it wait?"

Angela frowned. "We should talk about how this is affecting you. I know you are almost an adult now. I can't believe my baby is so grown up. But transferring schools your junior year isn't ideal ..."

"Transferring countries, transferring schools, transferring homes. Yeah, three life changes all at once is fantastic fun. Good thing I got a say on something like that before you pulled the trigger." His usually soft brown eyes were black as beetles. Angela couldn't tell if he was going to cry or break his cereal bowl against the wall.

The word "trigger" reignited her memory of the gut-wrenching night she and Melvin spent watching footage from the Vegas shooting. Lifeless heaps dotted the field where dancing and singing had occurred hours before. Jeremy and his friends were supposed to be there. They had bought tickets. Melvin and Angela had gone crazy with dread, barely speaking to each other, willing their phones to ring with a call or text from Jeremy. When he finally called them the next day, they were staring at the news like zombies, seeing the same clumps on the field in every version of footage, telling themselves, "No, that can't be him, any of those," but knowing it could be.

Jeremy and his friends had been on such a roll in the casino, flashing their fake IDs with zero push-back, that they completely forgot about the concert. And by the time they remembered, they were stopped on the street and ushered back inside by security personnel who explained there had been a shooting and they would need to stay inside until the authorities assured the hotels it was safe. While they waited, they drank themselves into a stupor and woke up with their heads pounding. When he finally called, Jeremy said he was sorry and started to cry. Angela and Melvin collapsed into each other's arms and sobbed. After a night's sleep, an out-of-touch president tweeted another out-of-touch tweet, prompting Melvin to announce, "It's time for me to go home." Angela agreed.

Angela physically recoiled, abruptly standing, her stomach in a knot.

"What?" Jeremy's eyes tracked her across the kitchen. "You said talk. Too much talk now?"

Angela opened the fridge. *Did I have lunch?* She couldn't recall. Her mind had gone fuzzy. The knot inside her throbbed for attention.

"I, um …" Angela closed the fridge and opened a cabinet. "Just hungry, I think." She found a tub of chocolate almonds, scooped out a handful, and threw them in her mouth. She gestured for Jeremy to continue. "So you're mad," she said around the almonds. "I get it." She took another handful and sat back down.

In the hot seat next to Jeremy, his unhappiness so evident, Angela recognized their decision to move was a selfish one. Melvin had sold his hack app for a ridiculous amount of money. The Canadian government offered him a stable job hack-testing its security systems. Though Angela had never regretted the all-consuming nature of her job, her priorities shifted after Vegas. She always loved Jeremy like a son, but she missed too many basketball games and parent-teacher meetings over the years. Trials and discovery deadlines were fixed and unforgiving. Her desire to put Jeremy's needs front and center became fierce. "I'm sorry we didn't consult you on moving, Jeremy."

He eyed her suspiciously. "Aren't you trying to lose weight?"

Angela swallowed. "What are you, my mother?" she said with a laugh.

He continued to glare, then picked up his spoon and took another bite.

"You could have stayed, but I admit we didn't offer that up as a solution." Angela placed a hand on his arm.

Jeremy continued munching, eyes fixed on the bowl in front of him.

"Surely you know how much we love you and want you with us." It came out more as a question than a statement. She crammed the last few almonds in her mouth and watched the pulse of muscle along Jeremy's jaw, marveling at the carefully groomed sideburn below his ear.

"Fine. Forget about it." When his ear bud went back in, Angela gave up. Somewhere inside that fortified wall was the kid who heard, "We love you," and itched for a reassuring bit of fleece.

chapter 13

BUOYED FROM ANOTHER MINUSCULE WEIGHT LOSS, ANGELA SAT IN THE SHAPESHIFTERS MEETING ROOM, READY FOR A NEW CHALLENGE.

"What did you do for movement?" Susan asked the group.

Blank stares. Finally, Angela said, "Trained for the 7k."

Susan nodded appreciatively and handed her a sticker.

Mina said, "Me too," and received a sticker.

"Make that three stickers," said Belinda.

"Yes, I hear the 7k training is off to a good start," Susan said while handing Belinda her sticker. "Tomorrow is session number two. Three kilometers of alternate running and walking. Anyone who has cleared it with her doctor is welcome to join in." There were some murmurs, so Susan raised her voice a little. "Who else tried something new to get moving this week?"

The buxom blond in back raised her hand. Susan nodded and the woman stood up. "I don't have a lot of time," she said. "I get up at quarter-to-six every morning so I can be at work by seven. That's when I get the most work done and can clear my projects before new ones hit." She paused to acknowledge the women nodding in the room. "So here's what I did this week. Blow drying takes a long time, I find. So I challenged myself to see how many squats I could do while I dried my hair. Turns out I can do sixty!" She gave the group a bright smile. "So I did three hundred squats this week. My butt feels spectacular." She turned around to demonstrate, smacking herself on the back pocket.

"That is quite something." Susan handed her a sticker. "Any compliments on your bum?" she asked.

Buxom Blond said, "Let's just say my husband noticed." She winked and sat down.

Susan had to speak over more murmuring and laughter. "Great job, group! Keep it up. Looking for ways to get in movement is a life skill."

She walked over to the whiteboard and drew a giant circle. "Now, eating balanced meals in the right portions is another life skill. Assume this circle is your plate. Who wants to draw a typical meal on it?"

Group members looked around at each other uneasily,

waiting to see if someone else would volunteer. Finally, Angela stepped up to the front and took Susan's marker. She drew a triangular shape on the top left, an apple on the bottom right, and a squiggly shape framing a small circle in the center of the plate.

"What's that thing in the middle?" Belinda asked.

"An egg," Angela said. "Fried with a little bit of olive oil."

"Thank you, Angela." Susan asked the group as Angela sat down again, "What do you guys think? Is this a proper meal with proper portions?"

"There's a lot of room left on the plate. What's the triangle?" a quiet-voiced woman with white curly hair asked.

"That's a scone," Angela explained. "I don't have them every day, but there's a cute little coffee place I walk to once or twice a week. They have fantastic scones. I eat an apple on my way there, and when I get home if I'm still hungry I have an egg. Hardboiled if there are any, but if not, fried."

"Isn't fried bad?" Belinda asked.

"She means sautéed, not fried, I think," Jo chimed in. Angela nodded.

"Is there anything missing?" Susan asked the group.

"A vegetable?" the curly-haired woman suggested.

"Another serving of fruit or a vegetable would fill up the plate nicely," Susan said, delighting the meek woman with a sticker. "Who knows a good rule of thumb to ensure your plate holds the right portion of the right foods?"

Buxom Blond offered, "The food chart is heavy on vegetables and fruits, so half the plate should be that. And the other half should be meat and starch?"

Susan handed her another sticker. "Yes, half your plate should be fruits and veggies, a quarter should be protein of some sort, and whole grains are recommended for the remaining quarter." She drew a few strawberries next to Angela's apple. Then she crossed out the scone and made little grain-dots around it. "Depending how the scone is made, it's a fine occasional indulgence, but oatmeal or high fiber toast is a better routine choice."

Jo scrunched up her nose at the oatmeal suggestion and raised her hand. "What has to be in a scone so we can pick that instead of oatmeal or toast?" She stuck out her tongue.

"Scones have a *lot* of butter. Butter is fine, but the calories will add up pretty quickly. Also, scones are often made with bleached wheat flour. There aren't a whole lot of nutrients in that. Add some oats or different types of grain flours, and you'll amp up the nutritional punch."

"What about adding blueberries?" Belinda offered. "Stand-Alone-Scones makes a killer blueberry scone." Murmurs of agreement filled the room.

"Adding fruit is another way to punch up the nutrients," Susan said. "I have some recipes I can share if you'd like. It sounds like this is a scone-loving group. To be honest," she said conspiratorially, "I make them most mornings. They're quite easy and inexpensive to make." Almost every arm shot up asking for the recipe. Susan counted the hands and took out her phone. She found the right file and pressed the print button. "You can pick it up on the way out today," she said. She concluded the meeting with a challenge to make at least one portion-correct plate per day for the following week.

As members found their way to the front desk for recipes, Mina and Angela talked about their week.

"I lost two pounds this week," Mina said with a ring of pride in her tone.

"That's so great!" Angela said. "Do you think it was the run we did?"

"Maybe. I am just more conscious, I think, of what goes in my mouth when I'm home."

"Yeah, me too. Ever since the feelings meeting, I am shocked how many times I catch myself eating for every reason except hunger."

Mina nodded.

Angela thought about her drive home and the McDonald's she would pass on the way. She had been craving French fries. And now that the weigh-in for the week was over, maybe she would treat herself. *Is that a reward or a comfort-eating craving?* her subconscious asked. And she realized Melvin would be in meetings all day, so she would face loneliness at home. A big comfort food trigger for her was loneliness. "What are you up to next?" Angela asked Mina, hoping for a diversion.

"I'm meeting a French teacher at the library. I want to surprise my daughter and learn some French. She's having a tough time with it at school."

That's just what Angela needed. Something new to learn. "Can anyone sign up for it?"

"Oh, yes. You should come! It's a group lesson. Focusing on conversation skills."

"Perfect." They stopped to collect their recipes and headed outside. "I'll drive."

Angela opened the car door for Mina, pausing while she sat, gathered some fabric overlapping the door's path, and pulled it inside. When her skirts settled and her seat belt was secured, Angela gently closed the door.

Buckling her own seat belt, Angela couldn't ignore the bump of fat against it. It was a smaller bump, but still. She checked herself in the rearview mirror for mascara smears. She realized Mina was attuned to her actions throughout the buckling and the mirror-checking, and felt painfully shallow, seated next to someone who presented the same faceless image to the world each day. Her cheeks burned. "Spring Mill Library?"

"Yes," Mina said. "I'll direct you."

On the way there, Angela drilled Mina on what she knew about this French lesson.

"It was an advertisement on the bus," Mina said. "That's all I know."

Angela wondered what kind of French class advertised on busses and fretted that she might be in way over her head.

"My daughter. She's in her third year of high school."

"My son too!" *Jeremy might be a similar age*, Angela thought. *A potential friend!*

Mina was quiet for a moment. "French is important in this country. I can see my Laila is having a tough time. I'd like to help her if I can."

"Right." Angela recalled her heated conversation with

Jeremy. "Like it isn't hard enough moving to a new country third year of high school."

"Turn left here." Mina pointed.

Angela turned onto a street marked Rue de Riviére and spotted the library up ahead. "What was it like for Laila school-wise? In Syria?"

"Turn left there in the parking lot," Mina said. Then after Angela parked, she continued, "It was not easy. She mastered all the subjects, but it was not completely acceptable for her to be attending school. The older she got, the more pressure she felt to quit and find a husband. It's one of the reasons we chose to leave." She looked out the window, unbuckling her seat belt. "No matter the risk." Her voice lacked conviction.

Angela nodded, unbuckled, and the two of them approached the library in silence for a few paces. "So you don't know anything about this French lesson?" Angela was concerned that her two years of high school French were baby steps compared to what she may be encountering. "It's for beginners at least. Right?"

Mina shrugged. They walked through the doors and followed signs to a stairwell down to the ground level. They pushed open a door with a glass window that had "French Lesson" on a piece of paper taped to it. Inside, they found a giant table made from six smaller tables pushed together. There were twelve people seated around it chattering enthusiastically. In French. Angela had no idea what they were saying. She looked at Mina, whose expression was unreadable. They sat in two chairs outside of the group, as there were no chairs free at the table. The instructor babbled something presumably in French while handing them a sign-up sheet. Angela detected there was a question in the babbling. The instructor waited a beat too long after they accepted the sign-up sheet.

Mina brought all her attention to the paper in front of her, grabbing the pen and giving off the impression she was about to put her name and email in the appropriate sections. The instructor kept his gaze enthusiastically tuned to Angela's confused face.

"*Je ne sais pas*," was all Angela could think to say. She used that phrase often in high school, a popular phrase among her classmates. There was a cacophony of laughter among the group at the table.

The instructor's expression turned from expectation to sudden comprehension. "Ah. This is intermediate French conversation class. *Mais bienvenue.*"

Mina's pen stopped scribbling mid–email address. Although she continued to look down at the paper, Angela felt they both understood exactly what to do at exactly the same time.

They excused themselves to use the washroom and then they bolted. In the library lobby, they bursted out laughing. Suppressed nervous giggles exploded into doubled-over, side-splitting laughter.

"Definitely not beginners," Angela said after a few calming breaths.

"Did you understand any of that?"

"It doesn't even sound French," said Angela. "I mean, I did pretty well in high school French but … it sounded alien, like deep southern twang meets rural Parisian kind of dialect."

Just then, the instructor came bounding up the stairs, frightening both of them. Mina jumped back two feet, and Angela's stomach lurched. "Excuse me," he said, focusing on Angela. "I did not mean to scare you off."

"Oh, we were just going to the washroom," Angela said. He looked at the sign above him that pointed to washrooms being downstairs.

"We were taking a minute here first, though," Angela added.

"Uh huh." The instructor was clearly not buying it. "Look, if you truly want to learn, you can just sit and listen for a while. Give it a week or two, and if you still can't utter a word in French, you can leave."

Angela noticed the instructor had not looked at Mina once during the conversation. "We didn't get a welcoming vibe," Angela said.

He narrowed his eyes at her, fixed in place as if deciding what to say. Finally, he threw up his arms and marched off down the stairs.

chapter

14

SUSAN GLANCED AT HER RINGING PHONE AS SHE UNLOCKED HER DOOR AND WALKED IN. It was Marty, the district manager. Why would he call her? Most ShapeShifter business was done by email. She desperately wanted the interim manager position and he knew it, so she answered right away.

"Hey, Susan. How's it going?"

She loathed his fake-nice voice, but it was easier to take on the phone than in person. Marty was disarmingly handsome—one of those men you felt like you might be flirting with even when you weren't. She had never seen him looking casual. He always wore a gray or navy suit, a trendy shirt with unusual colors or buttons, and a whimsically artful tie. It was not a look just anyone could pull off. "Hi, Marty. Just got back from my meeting. How are you?"

"Fine, fine. Meeting went well I assume? You're still one of the most popular leaders in the region."

The compliment made her stomach flutter. "Thank you. I do my best. Did you get my stats?" That's the only reason she could think of for his call. He reported to the company directors on Tuesday mornings and got antsy when he didn't have statistics from one of the more successful meetings by noon Monday.

"I did, thank you. Just a tiny thing I wanted to mention about the stats, actually."

"Tiny thing?" Susan's mind spun to Angela and her tricky weigh-in ruse. The other members seemed motivated by her rather than annoyed as Susan might have thought. Despite Angela's questionable need to lose weight, Susan appreciated her energy in the meetings. And she owed her big time for leading the first training session.

"Yes, you have one member on the roster who is awfully close to the low end of her BMI if I'm reading this correctly. Angela Marshall. Does that ring a bell?"

"Yes …" *Where's he going with this?* The numbers showed she had five pounds to lose. Surely, he didn't know about the loaded–back pockets maneuver.

"Does she have a goal weight?"

"Not yet." Sensitive to the fact that Angela may have a

food disorder, Susan had avoided bringing up the goal weight discussion. Once she reached whatever her goal weight was, she would be encouraged to graduate.

"Yes, well you might want to have that discussion sooner rather than later."

"May I ask why the focus on this particular member?" She swallowed against a wave of panic.

Marty laughed and cleared his throat. "Oh, you know how it is. Pressure from the directors to make our stats shine as much as we can. There might be a feature in the magazine about your meeting, and we don't want to draw attention to any … flaws, let's say."

"Well, that's good news. About the feature," Susan said. Phew. Maybe she'd dodged a bullet.

"Absolutely." Marty shifted into a tone drenched with artificial enthusiasm. "There's just one more tiny little kink we need to address as well."

Here it comes. Susan braced herself. She was motivated by criticism, but excessive criticism had the opposite effect for her. "I'm listening." She took a deep breath.

"Yes, well, one of the members called the home office."

Oh God. Member complaints were the worst. There would be a sit-down with her in the meeting and a *constructive* conversation about what she could improve upon.

Marty continued, "It seems they were looking for the ShapeShifters recipe for Crave-Killer Cookies."

The heat in Susan's face radiated slowly down her neck to her chest. When members complained they couldn't eat just one cookie without the whole package being consumed, she always recommended the Crave-Killers. They were full of filling ingredients but also delicious, so most members were able to stop with just two or three. Did someone ask her for it and she forgot to give it? She tried to remember. "Right. Those are a big help with binge-eaters," Susan said carefully.

"Yeaaahhh," Marty drawled. "The thing is, it's actually not a ShapeShifters recipe. We can't have leaders passing off recipes of their own as official recipes." He let this sink in. "You understand. We have our own nutritionists. We stand by recipes developed at the home office. Uniformity, you understand."

"I don't understand," Susan said. "Are you asking me to send you the recipe so you can run it by the nutritionists?"

"No, no …" Marty's voice lowered to a level not quite jovial. "Just um, stick to the official recipes when you are making recommendations. Push the products, eh? This week, coconut bars are on special. Sound good?"

Susan grimaced at the thought of pushing a bar full of chemicals on her members. A Snickers bar had more nutritional value than a ShapeShifters one. "So even if it helps members lose weight, I can't share my own recipes?"

"Riiiight," he drawled. "I knew you'd understand. Thanks, Susie, it's been great chatting with you." Before Susan could process the directive, he hung up.

What a twit. She stood numbly in her office looking through the window. She had a prime view of the one tree she and Lex planted when they moved in. Every year, they had to buy another strand of lights for it at Christmas time. The branches rewarded them by multiplying year after year.

She still had her jacket on and her purse in hand. She let out a long breath that came out in gasps. She was rattled. Since she started at ShapeShifters, her record had been exemplary. Now there was a blemish. She could feel her promotion slipping away.

Over the desk hung her teaching diploma. Next to it was her Masters in Education certificate. Fixating on them usually quelled her anxiety, but they also reminded her of failure. She never pursued her Ph.D. as planned. After her first maternity leave, she elected to stay home with Caleb. It felt right, focusing all her energy on motherhood, so after Kimberly and Ester, she put her professional goals on hold some more. When she turned to ShapeShifters for help with the five pounds she gained with each baby, she enjoyed the camaraderie of other adults she found in the meetings. It filled a void, allowing her human connection beyond the friends she made through the kids. When she reached her goal, ShapeShifters offered her a job. One day a week. It was a toe in the door. A distraction from full-time parenting.

The certificates now accused her from the wall. She was capable of more. But after raising three kids, her passion for education lost its luster. She knew she was overqualified for ShapeShifters, but the work was rewarding. With each pound lost, and with each member achieving her goal, Susan's confidence in her choice strengthened. She was good at this. She would be a manager some day. Once Ester was off to university and Susan had even more time on her hands.

She turned on her computer and opened the file

renamed "It's Not Complicated." Each recipe had a proven track record. She held her finger over the delete key.

Something about pursuing the perfect recipe for a given struggle drew the circle in her life closer to complete. She recalled the various hats she'd worn after teaching: Motherhood (still working on the Ester issues); Marathon Runner (she completed a few but never with a sense of mastery); Homeless Shelter Volunteer (the cycle of despair depressed her); and ShapeShifters Leader (more fulfilling than any of those, if she was honest). She saw her life as an exploratory circle with the top link missing. The feeling suffocated her when she imagined an obituary someday: "Mother, giving volunteer, former teacher …" Were any of these things truly her life's work?

She was getting closer with the recipes. All concept of time evaporated when she cooked, baked, dumped ideas that didn't work, and wrote down ones that did. The appreciation and success of members who tried her recipes put her closer to that thing she lacked. But it wasn't enough to get her promoted. The path to corporate nutritionist was a dead end without a dietician degree. She shuddered at the thought of immersing herself in a science-laden program, far from the face-to-face interactions that inspired her.

Taking her hand off the delete key, she sat back in her office chair. Gazing out the window, she tracked the slow descent of bright orange and red leaves. Her reflection, lost in the window's glare, flared with color as each leaf drifted by. She set down her purse and took a key from the inside zipper. Next she unlocked a bottom desk drawer.

From a collection of upright file folders, she withdrew a mirror. Her dad convinced her of its *magic powers*, incorporating it into the same bedtime story every night. He may not have known any others, but it didn't matter because she loved that one. It was about a little girl searching for a prince. The mirror found its way to the girl every time, though the story of how it came into her hands changed nightly. And when the mirror arrived, she would look into it, hungry for a reflection that might lead her across a prince's path. The princess's reflection changed, as if by magic, as she encountered adventure after adventure. Sometimes she was a powerful queen, a jeweled crown sparkling on her head, with a kingdom to rule. Next she might be an aggressive barrister with a dark bob, serious lips arguing successfully for the neediest of her clients. Other times, she would see a vague outline of her face with a halo of blond adding to the fuzziness. That was the face of pursuits, her dad explained. When she saw that face, she needed another adventure to get her closer to her destiny.

She lost her dad too young. Years of drinking too heavily led to an unexpected heart attack. On the day of the wake, she found a mirror much like her dad had described in a box marked "Toys" in the attic. She took it out of the box with deep longing and expectation, but the reflection was nothingness. She turned the mirror this way and that, but no face appeared in it. Its surface had a lacquer-like coating that prevented her from seeing anything.

She pulled the mirror out of the drawer and looked into it again. The same shimmer rejected her image. She told herself it would be the same no matter who looked into it. That's just what the mirror looked like. It was a trick mirror of some kind, something bought at a dime store decades ago. But she had never been quite sure. And anyway, she could not face the prospect of losing the story that connected her father to her own destiny.

chapter

15

SUSAN HAD A SENSE OF FOREBODING AS SHE PULLED INTO THEIR AGREED-UPON TRAINING LOCATION. But when she saw the gang finishing up the warm-up exercises on their own, she was happy.

"You warmed up! Excellent." She grabbed a bag from the back seat and hustled toward Mina, Angela, Belinda, and Jo. They wore exactly what they wore last time. "Let me go over the plan here. Huddle up."

Jo had already started to overheat. She unzipped her ski jacket as they formed a circle around Susan. Belinda bounced on her toes, eager to get started.

"Today's distance is 3k," Susan began. She looked around at the blank faces. "You did 2k last week, right?" They nodded in unison. "Okay, we're adding a kilometer but it will feel different here. Instead of pavement, we are on a dirt path, softer on your feet. The trees will protect us from the wind a bit. And there will be a fair amount of dog walkers to distract us."

"I don't like big dogs," Mina said quietly.

"Okay, we will keep you in the middle of the group, then," Susan reassured Mina. "If we see any big dogs, we will intercept them so they can't pester you."

Mina's head, aimed in Susan's direction, neither nodded yes nor shook no.

"I'll run in front of Mina," Belinda said, eager to get started.

"I'll run behind her," said Jo.

"Don't worry," Susan said to Mina. "Angela and I will stay at your sides." She peered into the screen where Mina's eyes should be. "You okay, Mina?"

"Yes," Mina said with the same quiet voice.

"I have a surprise for you guys," Susan said, reaching into the grocery bag. She pulled out a large pink and green T-shirt with "ShapeShifters" written on the front. "This one's for you, Jo." She handed her the cheerful lump of fabric. "Let me know if it's too big."

"Woohoo!" Jo said. "Team shirts!" She turned the back of it so everyone could see "Jo" written there.

"You are all winners, accomplishing training number one and showing up for number two," Susan said. "If we're going to train as a team, we might as well look like one." She handed out the rest of the shirts and everyone tried them on.

"I'm totally wearing mine now," said Belinda, squeezing the shirt on over her jacket. The rest followed suit. Mina put in extra effort to keep her head-covering on straight while squishing the T-shirt down over her burqa. Jo waddle-ran back to the car to ditch her ski coat before rejoining the others.

"Okay, same drill as last week. We run one minute, walk two minutes. Next week that will change to one-and-ones, so enjoy it! I have the path all measured so I know where to go. Let's all try to stay together, okay?" Susan said. She started to jog in place.

The rest of them jogged in place with her. Then Belinda took off down the path and Susan fell in behind her. "Let's stay together, Belinda." Belinda looked back and jogged in place a bit until Mina and the others caught up.

They passed a little cluster of dogs with the walker holding multiple leashes on their way into the trees. Susan led them off the main path on to a narrower one, where trees and tall weeds lined the edges. A sheltie appeared in front and Mina squeaked. The other four closed in around her. The sheltie stopped to sniff at Susan then took off into the woods, its owner sauntering along unconcerned a few meters behind it. "You still okay?" Susan said, turning to Mina.

Mina nodded, and they followed the path in and out of trees. Off-leash dogs, big and small, appeared randomly and without incident. After what seemed like forever, Susan called out the first walk break.

The path took them on to a soft carpet of pine needles as they walked, large conifers forming a cozy canopy above them. Angela said to Mina, "Ever have a pet?"

Mina shook her head. "Animals are not pets where I come from."

"Ever been bitten?"

"No," she said. "But my uncle was attacked by a wild cat. He got an infection and died." Angela made an appalled face.

"Don't worry," Jo said as they started running again. "There are no wild cats around these parts, and if there were, they would not attack a group."

Mina seemed to relax as the run neared completion. She held her skirt up with one hand like she did last time to keep from tripping. But Angela noticed she let her skirts fall anytime a man came into view. On the last one-minute run, Mina's toe caught a root and she stumbled, flopping onto the ground head first.

"Oh my God, are you okay?" Susan asked.

Mina's hood was jostled so the screen was off center. She sat up and tried to right it. There was a small rock where Mina's head had landed, and Susan noticed a wet place on her hood.

"Are you bleeding?"

Mina reached her hand to her head and felt the wet place. "I … I'll be fine. I should go home now," she said.

"Let me have a look," Jo said. "I'm a nurse."

Mina shook her head, "Not out here. Not in public."

Jo crouched beside Mina, watching the wet spot on

Mina's headscarf slowly expand. She looked up at Susan, her expression something between 'help' and 'what the fuck?'

Susan knelt next to Jo. She saw Jo's concern immediately. "Mina," Susan said, "If you can't let us assess how serious your head wound is, we will have to call an ambulance."

"No ambulance," Mina said and started to stand up. Jo and Susan each grabbed an arm to help her, but as soon as she was standing, they felt her swoon and helped her gently back to the ground.

"Listen," Jo said. "This path is pretty wide. I'll drive my car in and take Mina to the hospital." Mina held up a hand in protest. "They will assess you in private at the hospital," Jo said. The four of them waited anxiously, Mina helpless on the ground. Finally, Mina nodded and said okay.

Once Mina was strapped into Jo's car, the car sped off, tires squealing.

"Well that was something," Belinda said after they left. "Is the training over?"

Susan looked at her watch. "I'm sorry it was cut a little short. We had a half kilometer left to go. We'll make up for it next week." She placed her hand on Belinda's arm in a gesture of sympathy.

"Screw that," Belinda said. "I'm running back! See you guys at the meeting." And she sprinted away like a bull fresh from the gates.

Angela turned to Susan. "She's a keener, that one. She was ahead of us the whole time last week."

"Hmm," Susan said. "Next week I'll come up with a plan that accommodates all levels."

The two of them walked back toward the parking lot, silently at first. They passed a playful black lab who danced up to them and sniffed. After that, a cluster of poodle mixes pitter-pattered by them. A group of teenagers walking just ahead of them stopped to stare at each others' phones and laughed.

As they neared a wooden fence bordering the parking lot, Susan turned to Angela. "Can we talk a minute? It's a ShapeShifters matter, but it's so harried at the meetings, it might be best to chat here."

"Sure." Angela stopped, her eyes brightly scanning Susan's.

"We never really talked about the way you … became a ShapeShifters member."

Angela's eyes fell to her toes. "I'm sorry," she said. "I know you have your rules. It's just I really needed help, and I don't think it's fair the program only helps if you're, well, almost hopelessly fat." Before Susan could explain, Angela added, "I get it. The fatter you are, the longer it takes to get thin, so registering mostly obese members is good for the company's bottom line. But I feel like you're missing a whole demographic of women who struggle constantly to keep their weight stable and need help with the basics like everyone else."

Susan looked down at her shoes. "Maybe you're right about that." She heard Marty's voice in her head: *Push our products.* She reminded herself that without the revenue, the company would not be able to help people. That was the focus: to stay in business to help. "The next step for you would be to set a goal weight," she began. Remembering their first conversation at the scale, when Angela mentioned a weight range where she felt great in her clothes, Susan prodded, "You had a goal in mind when we first spoke, I think. Are you there yet?"

They were standing at the fence now. Angela sat on the top rung and considered the question. "Not yet, but I feel better about my weight now that I know I'm getting help. It's a process, like you said."

"Okay." Susan sat down beside her. "I'm glad you are feeling good about your process. Can you do me a favor and come up with a goal weight before our next meeting?"

"Sure," Angela said, uncomfortable about having to put a number on her end game. "But why?"

Susan let out a deep sigh. "Let me be honest with you, Angela. You mentioned your appreciation of company rules from a 'revenue-making' perspective. I'm getting some pressure to move you toward graduation. That's what happens when you make your goal weight."

Angela frowned. "Will I get to come to the meetings after I graduate?"

"Well, in theory you won't need the meetings then." Susan saw the disappointment hit Angela's face. "But you can keep coming for a reduced fee." Oh boy. That would take some creative bookkeeping.

"Okay, I'll think about it," Angela said. "Can I ask you a question?"

"Sure, anything." Perhaps this would be resolved more easily than Susan had thought.

"First of all, your scones were crazy good. Thanks for that. I haven't had a coffee shop one since!"

"I'm glad to hear it." Another feel-good moment Susan would lose if she couldn't share her own recipes.

"Melvin and I—that's my husband—go out to eat a lot. Sometimes that leads to bar-hopping, late-night snacking, and excessive drinking," Angela confided sheepishly. "I used to just drink lots of liquids the next day when I'd had one of those excess nights—tea, coffee, soups, smoothies, kind of a detox of sorts—and that would seem to set me right for the rest of the week. But that routine doesn't work for me anymore. Is it crazy to have a detox strategy like that?" She looked at Susan pleadingly. "And do you have any that work for you?"

Susan thought about her Me-Tox smoothie recipe. Then she thought of Marty—she should be pushing the ShapeShifters smoothie powders. Susan had tried the coffee flavored one once. It wasn't bad. But something in her couldn't push another product containing artificial flavors, preservatives, and salt. "Let me come up with a couple of ideas and email you, okay?" she finally said. This way it would be from Susan to Angela as friends and not ShapeShifters leader to member. No rules broken.

"Great!" Angela said. "That would be so awesome, thank you!" They took out their phones and exchanged contact information. As Susan walked back to her car, she wondered if she had taken a big risk, befriending a member for the sake of her health.

chapter

16

BY THE TIME MINA WAS RELEASED FROM THE HOSPITAL, SHE KNEW HER DAUGHTER WOULD BE HOME.

"Don't be a stranger," Jo said, dropping Mina off at her front door. "Do you need help inside, Mina?"

"I'll be fine. Thank you for the ride." She was anxious to get inside.

"You have someone to keep an eye on you? Just because the doctor didn't think it's a concussion doesn't mean it won't turn into one."

"Yes, I live with my daughter and husband," Mina assured her.

"And you'll keep ice on it?" Jo pressed.

"Yes, yes, I'll go straight to the freezer when I am inside. Thank you."

"Okay, then. I know where you live now, so if you don't show up for the meeting, I'm going to hunt you down." Jo wagged her finger.

Mina laughed. "Goodbye. See you soon."

Inside, her daughter was already home. Mina carefully removed her wrappings, T-shirt, and shoes before finding Laila in the kitchen, cooking rice. "What are you making?"

"Just starting the rice for you," Laila said. "I was hungry."

"Thank you." Mina opened the freezer door in search of ice. She saw a bag of frozen onions and decided that would work.

"What happened to you?" Laila's eyes zoned in on the lumpy gash marking Mina's temple.

Mina placed the bag over it and sighed. "I've been running with some women from ShapeShifters." She pulled out a chair from the table against the wall and sat, leaning on her elbow to keep the bag in place. "I tripped."

Laila looked more closely at her mother, taking in her running tights and dry-fit top. "Since when do you run?"

"This is only my second time. I didn't know if I'd like it. Or if I could do it. But it's fun." Mina noted the incredulity in her daughter's eyes. "Exercise is supposed to be fun," she said defensively.

"Well, cracking your head open doesn't sound fun to

me." Laila checked the rice, replaced the lid, and turned off the burner. "Where's the meat? I'll make dinner."

Mina pointed to the refrigerator and sighed gratefully. As Laila rifled through the items in the fridge, Mina took in her daughter's youthful figure. She was wearing tight black pants with a loosely buttoned flannel shirt, but as she bent over, her slender frame shone through. Her chest pressed snugly against her tank top, visible underneath the flannel. Her long, glossy hair swept gracefully across her back as she removed a package of ground lamb from the fridge.

"How was school today?"

"It was okay." Laila fished out a large skillet from beneath the oven.

"I noticed you weren't wearing your burqa the other day." Mina eyed Laila carefully for her reaction.

Laila's back stiffened. She paused with the skillet mid-air. Then she set it down gently. "You've been spying on me?" She kept her back turned.

"Don't change the subject. How long have you been abandoning your traditional clothes the minute you leave the house?"

Laila turned the burner on and dumped the meat into the pan. She turned around and shot her mother an agitated look on her way to the waste basket. Then she turned her back to Mina again, taking a spatula out of the drawer next to the stove and breaking up the meat in the skillet. "The second day of school," she finally said, stabbing at the meat. "After I realized how backward it is to cover ourselves up so much."

Mina's throat tightened. She felt the words like daggers. But she needed to know more, so she clawed through the pain, trying to focus on this beautiful creature, her flesh and blood, standing before her. She felt wounded still from her daughter's insistence on walking alone to the bus stop. Her pride fed the anger inside her, but she stuffed it back down.

Mina moved the onions to a colder spot to quell the stab in her temple. "What happened on the first day?" She wanted to say, *What happened to cause you to form this conceited opinion, to opt for flamboyance over modesty?* but didn't.

Laila stabbed at the meat some more. She turned slightly to look at her mother and said, "Did it ever occur to you how much easier running would be without your burqa?"

"That has nothing to do with—"

"It has everything to do with it." Laila turned and faced her mother, ferocity in her voice. "We don't sit in one spot and cook all day in school. We go to lockers, we carry stacks of books from class to class, we stand up in front of our peers and give reports on our work, we interact with other students to collaborate on projects, we learn how to solve problems while also socializing and tapping into what's going on in the world." Laila brushed a lock of hair from her eye that stubbornly clung to her face. "The burqa hinders all these things. And for what? Modesty? So some boy doesn't look down my shirt? That's part of being a teenager, Mom. I check out the boys too. That's part of the socializing process." She paused to see if her mother was listening.

Mina was gathering her thoughts.

"And when I hear you are running, *running* in your

burqa with other women and injure yourself in the process, that just proves my point. Don't you see how ridiculous it is to maintain this tradition for the sake of modesty alone?" She spat the word "tradition" like it was snake venom. Having finished her rant, she assessed the meat and saw that it was brown enough. She turned the heat to low and added some spices and a little water, stirring.

Mina wondered when religion became tradition for her daughter. "Are you done?" A calm had returned to Mina's voice. She would control this conversation.

Laila said, "If you listened, *really* listened, then yes, I'm done."

"Then tell me. What happened on the first day of school?"

chapter

17

SUSAN, WORRIED ABOUT MINA, DISTRACTED HERSELF WITH RECIPE CREATION. She was eager to develop some smoothie and soup recipes to address Angela's need to detox.

Detox. What a lark. The whole world seemed to be convinced that a "juice cleanse" or "liquid diet" would clean out your system and wash all the fat away like magic. No one wanted to face the realities of what we put into our bodies regularly and the miraculous detox that happened naturally. Junk in, junk out. It wasn't complicated. Still, Susan knew all too well that substituting something nutritious and filling for something masquerading as food was the fastest way to change a tired, lumpy body shape into an energized one.

Oh dear. Reaching into her cabinet for the blender, she realized she forgot to ask Angela for the specifics of her liquefied routine. How could Susan fashion alternatives for her without knowing what *wasn't* working? She smacked herself on the head. Finding her phone, she pulled up Angela's contact information. She pressed the email icon and wrote:

> Hi, Angela.
>
> Can you give me an idea of what your 'detox' day looks like? That will help me come up with more productive alternatives. Just give me a scenario or two of what you would drink at each meal, ingredients of the drink, and approximately what time you would consume each meal/drink. Do you exercise on those days? Information on the type and length of exercise on those days would also be helpful.
>
> Best,
> Susan

While she waited, Susan fired up her computer and searched her "It's Not Complicated" file for soups and smoothies she had already recommended with success. The Chicken Suav Blanc soup was a big hit with some of her more gourmet members who enjoyed coq au vin regularly. She clicked print on that one. She had two smoothie recipes: the green Me-Tox one she invented for Ester (not that Ester would drink something Mom-recommended) and a tropical smoothie she invented for members returning from tropical vacations who still craved their piña coladas.

Susan's phone pinged. Angela had already replied.

Hi Susan,

Great to hear from you! So excited to see what you can come up with. When I was working, I would drink a SlimQuick for breakfast. Then for lunch, around 1:00 or so, I'd walk over to the food court and grab a smoothie from Fro Yo Fruit—usually a yogurt pineapple coconut banana one, but sometimes I'd shake it up with a banana peanut butter & chocolate one. At home I would have a can of chunky soup or if I had made vegetable pistou on the weekend, I would have a bowl of that. Not gonna lie, I'd have a glass or two of wine as well and totally count it as liquid. :) Still I would always lose a pound or two and my stomach would feel smaller so I'd eat less the next few days. Thoughts?

Gratefully Yours,
Angela

Susan read the email again and tried to picture Angela's typical day. She emailed her right back:

> Hi again,
>
> Any workouts or recreational exercise in your week?
>
> Susan

The response came less than a minute later.

> No formal exercise when I was working. Maybe the odd aerobics class with a friend once in a blue moon. But I was on the go all day, between meetings and court hearings. Not kidding. I still walk a lot in my new life here, but mostly from pub to pub. LOL. Oh and the 7k training is my only 'legit' exercise right now.

Susan typed back right away.

> Okay, I get the picture now. Stay tuned and thank you.

Angela fired back a smiley face emoji.

So her detox day was SlimQuick (chemicals, added vitamins, and sugar), and her smoothie was also loaded with sugar and probably full-fat dairy in the yogurt. Lots of trans fats from modified palm oil, Susan noted. So that's two fruits at most by lunch. And the only vegetables were in the soup at night. Not much protein either. Angela was probably too busy to notice how hungry she was. Typical for a young woman at the start of her career. The challenge would be coming up with simple but just-as-delicious alternatives that would keep her full with her current activity level.

Just then, the door banged open and Ester lumbered in, slamming the door behind her.

Susan looked at her watch. "What are you doing home?"

Ester's face was red. The skin under her eyes was puffy from crying. Angry tears, judging by her expression. "I got suspended!" Ester screeched, stomping up the stairs before Susan could react.

Ester? The academic, athletic, MVP marvel, suspended? What on earth …

Susan's phone rang. She started to click off the sound and let the voice mail pick up when she saw it was Marty. Twice in one week. Wow. Maybe he was calling to say her meeting was top in the province. Maybe she was one step closer to getting a manager position. Maybe she could write her own ticket after this, even push for changing up the food products, targeting the demographic Angela represented, re-vamping the suggested recipes …

"Hi, Marty. This is a surprise," she answered.

"Susan." It wasn't his artificially pleasant voice. It was a serious voice. "What is going on with the 7k race program?"

His accusatory tone made Susan recoil. Where was he going with this? He was aware that she volunteered her time training with members who chose to participate in the corporate event. She didn't get paid extra, and she provided shirts at her own expense. She had received nothing but praise for this in past staff meetings. "Well, it's going quite well. We had our second session yesterday. I managed to counsel that member you were concerned about at the same time, and she is thinking about her goal weight—"

"You haven't seen it," Marty said.

"Seen what?"

"The Muslim woman on the ground. Bunch of gals in ShapeShifters shirts standing over her. Someone's got it on video and the damn thing's gone viral."

chapter

18

LAILA DECIDED NOT TO TELL HER MOTHER WHAT HAPPENED THE FIRST DAY OF SCHOOL. Her mother sat waiting for an answer at the small table in their cramped kitchen, clutching a bag of frozen onions to her head. This image of helplessness sickened Laila. She was stronger than her mother. She would adapt to whatever this country threw at her. But hurting her mother was not an option. She had been through too much. They had all been through too much.

To stall, Laila found the teakettle and filled it with water. "How about some tea?" Her mother's grateful smile was disarming. Laila reminded herself to stay strong. While the kettle heated up, she set out two small cups and the tea her mother liked. She opened the box of black tea, the *zouhourat* kind, and smelled. Its hibiscus flower scent made her think of gardens and sunshine. And peace.

"Can I smell?" Mina asked.

Laila held the open box under Mina's nose. She watched her mother breathe in the aroma and visibly relax, the tension in her jaw evaporating.

Laila brought the cups of freshly brewed tea to the table and sat in a chair opposite her mother, facing the only window. Sunlight streamed in, catching floating bits of dust that made Laila think of angels. They each took a sip simultaneously, and Laila felt the *zouhourat* melt the tension from her neck. She brought her hand to her shoulder just under her ear and rested it there. "The first day went well," Laila lied.

Mina frowned in disbelief, so Laila quickly continued. "There was a teacher there to greet me when I arrived. Our sponsors must have set it up. She was nice. She wore a green dress that clashed with her red hair. Her necklace reminded me of a shoelace with thin pieces of shell attached."

Mina smiled.

Laila paused, thinking. After watching a few leaves sink to the bottom of her cup, she continued. "Her name was Madame Gamelin. She showed me my class schedule and took me around to introduce me to the teachers at the end of each class. She also pointed out students she knew and made a point of soliciting their support in case I needed help when she wasn't around."

Laila remembered the enthusiasm in some of the students' faces when they met her and the fake sincerity in others that barely hid their indifference. She could see they were distracted by her burqa and would't look directly at her. They mostly watched Mme. Gamelin, their eyes gazing past Laila like she might be found floating just below the ceiling.

"Were the students nice?" Mina prompted. "Did you make any friends?"

"Not at first," Laila said, hoping to imply she had friends now. "It was hard to connect. We have nothing in common, really, except school." She grappled for something positive to say. "We collaborate on projects, and that has helped."

"You mentioned activities before," Mina said. "Did you join any teams or clubs?"

At this, Laila flinched. To cover up her reaction she blew on her tea. But Mina was no fool.

"Something happened when you tried to join, didn't it?" Her arms stiffened, ready to pounce on whoever quashed her daughter's innocent spirit.

"Chill, Mom. Nothing like that," Laila said. She was drawing nearer to the truth. Uncomfortably close.

Laila tried fogging her mother with details. "I looked into some of them. There was Chess Club, which looked interesting but everyone there knew the game already. I didn't want to be the only one learning. It was mostly boys. They were nice to me." Laila hoped Mina wouldn't take this to mean others weren't nice to her. "Chess Club meets at lunch in the basement. It kind of smells funny down there. Damp and dreary."

Mina nodded. "You've never liked rainy days."

Laila took another sip of tea.

Her mother made a gesture to continue.

"Um … let's see. There was field hockey, volleyball, and track. Nothing resembling cricket. They have baseball and golf in the spring, so maybe …" She didn't finish the sentence that could only end in a lie. "Field hockey is fast. I showed up for one tryout," Laila continued quickly. She took another sip, hoping she could wrap up the subject. "It wasn't for me."

"Why not?"

The question she had hoped to avoid. "It's fast. You have to run with a stick." *The burqa got in the way,* she didn't say. "I found it awkward."

"So you didn't make the team?"

Laila thought about the paper posted outside the gym and her refusal to look at it. "I didn't go to all the tryouts."

They sat quietly for a moment. Laila drained the last drop of her tea and hoped her account of Day One at school would satisfy her mother. But before she could get up to do the dishes, Mina placed a hand on her arm to stop her. "Did they make fun of you?" Her mother's eyes held tears ready to drop. Mina moved the onions away from her head and waited patiently for Laila to answer her question.

This was the part Laila could not tell her mother. It would add too much pain. Maybe some day when they were all settled she would tell her, but not now. She didn't want her freedom to dress like the others linked to a rashly made decision. A decision born of humiliation. "No, of course not. But my burqa got in the way." *Because it did make tryouts harder, yes*, she did not say. She left out the divisive wall it created between her and her peers.

Through the window, Laila watched her dad's car pull into the driveway, prompting her to stand and clear the teacups. "Dad's home."

Mina got up too, letting her hair fall over the bump near her face. She put the onions back in the freezer.

chapter

19

SUSAN REALIZED SHE HAD BEEN ON THE PHONE WITH MARTY FOR SEVERAL MINUTES AND SHE HADN'T TAKEN IN ANYTHING HE'D SAID. Something about Mina's fall, and the Internet, and a publicity nightmare. Susan's mind was on Ester upstairs. When Marty took a breath, Susan seized the opportunity. "I am sorry, Marty. I'm going to have to call you back."

"But—" she heard him say as she hung up. She turned the sound off and left the phone in her office.

Upstairs, Ester was feverishly texting. Her face, flustered and sad when she entered the house, was now fiery with anger. She looked up when her mother entered and shut off her phone quickly, placing it between her leg and her unmade bed.

Susan did nothing to quell Ester's concerns that she might take her phone. Pulling out the desk chair, she sat across from Ester. The bedroom wall, a mural of pastel pixies, snagged Susan's attention. She paused and breathed, laden with nostalgia. *When did this happen?* Susan wondered. The real world crowding out the imaginary. "Did you say *suspended*?"

"Yes." Ester stared daggers into Susan's eyes. "Two weeks. And you have to meet with the principal." She grabbed her backpack from atop her desk, fished a yellow piece of paper out of it, and handed it to her befuddled mother. "Here."

Susan glanced at it. The words "Suspension Notice" crossed the top, and at the bottom was a handwritten message requesting a phone call to arrange a meeting. "What on earth happened?"

"It was a misunderstanding." Ester's hands cast about wildly as she spoke. "I was talking to my friends. Just talking. No one else's business. Apparently, some guy overheard part of the conversation and thought I made a racial slur or something."

"Racial slur?" Susan was so shocked she had to say it to process it. Was her daughter capable of such a thing? She had her arrogant moments, but she was certainly not raised to be insensitive to others.

"Like I said, I don't know what he thinks he heard, but it was a private conversation."

"What did the principal say?"

"That they were investigating, but whatever that guy thinks I said was serious enough that I need to spend some time at home thinking about my actions." Ester's lip curled into a snarl. Then she looked down at her lap and sniffed.

Susan handed Ester a tissue. The notion her daughter may have actually said something cruel or mean hit her hard. "Who was the target of the slur?" Susan tried to think which of Ester's friends had a different skin color. There were a few, but Susan couldn't imagine Ester saying anything negative about them. They were all linked by school sports. They played on teams together, hung out at cafés after practice, talked over the games analytically, encouraged each other to work harder, and offered to do drills to help each other. At least, this is what Susan observed while shuttling the girls to practices and events.

"You don't know her. She's new. I barely know her."

So this girl was not one of her gang. "Does the kid who overheard something have a grudge against you of some kind?"

"I don't know." Ester used her breathy, you-are-so-annoying tone of voice that Susan decided to ignore. "He's new too."

"Well." Susan realized this was as far as she was going to get with Ester and her version. "Do your homework. I'll call the principal and set up a meeting, which you will be coming to." She emphasized the last part with dagger eyes. "If you are truly suspended, I will arrange for assignments, tests, and extra credit so you will spend the time working and not staring at your phone."

"You're not going to take it?" Ester changed her tone, suddenly respectful. "My phone?"

"Not until I know what the heck is going on."

Relief transformed Ester's face into the kind, innocent one Susan wanted to believe was real.

"Speaking of." Ester took out her phone and pulled up a Facebook meme. "What's going on here. Is this you?" She handed the phone to Susan after enlarging the video and pressing play.

Susan watched as Mina tripped and fell in a heap of fabric, over and over again, ending with the rest of the group crowding around her. Filling the screen were the words, "ShameShifter workout." Susan was horrified. She tapped the screen to watch it again. It was worse the second time. Then she looked at the comments below and saw it had been shared 25,000 times. "Oh my God."

"There are other versions. Some would be funny if they weren't so mean. Is that one of your members?"

"Yes." Susan moved to the bed next to Ester, staring at Mina's frozen image, vulnerable on the ground. With her running pals standing over her, backs to the camera, you couldn't see the concern on their faces.

chapter 20

MINA KNOCKED ON KELLY'S DOOR AND WAITED, CRADLING A TINY PUMPKIN IN THE CROOK OF HER ARM, FROZEN HANDS CONCEALED BY HER SLEEVES. The day had turned gray and gloomy, bringing a damp harshness to the cold.

Kelly opened the door promptly, ushering Mina inside. She noticed the pumpkin straight away. "What do you have there?"

"Just a little gift for your kindness." Mina held it out. "I've been seeing these all over the place. They are decorative and edible."

Kelly took the little pumpkin and twirled it around in her hands, scrutinizing each angle. Delight settled into her eyes. "Thank you. It's cute." She set the tiny pumpkin on the kitchen table, where it seemed lonely, Mina thought, but in a cheerful way. Kelly poured coffee into two cups then gestured with her chin for Mina to sit.

Mina removed her shoes and put them on the rack. "What game are we playing today?"

"What game would you like to play?" Kelly's eyes lit up.

Mina did not expect a choice but found she had an answer. "Chess!"

Kelly frowned. "Hmmm, I don't have that one. Why on earth would you want to play that game? It takes forever."

Mina looked down at her coffee, disappointed. "My daughter is interested in the game. I thought it might be something we could play together after I learn."

"Tell me about your daughter." Kelly took a sip of coffee, brushing at a stray crumb on the table.

"She is beautiful. And smart. She is doing well in school but she hasn't found an activity that works for her yet. She thought she might like chess, but …"

"But what?" Kelly, who had been staring appreciatively at the pumpkin, fixed her fierce eyes on Mina.

"Oh. It's probably nothing." Mina found a crumb of her own to brush at on the table. "But she tried out for a few sports teams. I've never seen her so discouraged."

"Mmhmm." Kelly got up from her chair and walked to the sink, then walked back. Mina noticed she didn't have her cane. Kelly sat back down and asked abruptly, "She wears one of those hijabs, does she?"

Mina stifled a gasp, grateful Kelly couldn't see the hurt she felt. She reminded herself that Kelly was an older woman and deserved deference. "She used to." She could see Kelly was unsatisfied with the answer.

Kelly appeared ready to launch an interrogation, but she seemed to think better of it. "Ever play checkers?"

Mina laughed with relief. "I have not."

Kelly sprang up, disappearing down the hallway.

Mina heard rustling sounds like cabinet doors opening and closing. "Do you need help?"

"Heavens no," Kelly shouted from the other room. "Been resting my knee. Feels like new now." A few minutes later she shuffled back into the kitchen with a box. Despite her careful gait, she did seem stronger. She plopped the box onto the table, sat, and began taking out red and black plastic coins. She stopped for a minute and gave Mina a stern look. "You're not going to stop coming, are you?"

Her vulnerability warmed Mina's heart. "I won't abandon you." She reached across the table and laid her hand on Kelly's arm. "We're friends now."

Kelly nodded curtly, carefully unfolding a board onto the table. Then she placed all the black coins on her side. She gave Mina a "your turn" gesture with her chin.

Mina took the red coins and set them up similarly on her end of the board, glancing at Kelly periodically to make sure she had it right. When finished, she had three rows of checkers.

Without explaining the game, Kelly moved one of her checkers onto a diagonal space in Mina's direction.

Mina did the same.

Kelly smiled approvingly and moved another checker toward Mina.

Mina did the same.

The third time Kelly moved, she made a show of hopping her checker over Mina's, landing in a blank space on Mina's side. Then she took the checker she hopped over and put it on her side of the table, off the board.

Mina looked around for a similar move and found one. She jumped over one of Kelly's checkers, capturing the coin with relish. If Kelly could see her face, she would see her smiling from ear to ear.

In the end, they counted all the kidnapped checkers. Kelly had the most. She won. Mina didn't have to ask.

"You catch on fast. Maybe you *can* handle chess." Kelly winked, placing the folded board back in the box. "Chess has a similar board, but the pieces are different. Each moves in a different way. There's a king and queen on each side, with an army of other pieces. The winner puts the king in such a tough place, he has nowhere else to go."

"Like a war."

Kelly studied Mina as she thought about this. "Is everything a war to you?"

Mina took a minute to decide whether they knew each other well enough that she could tease the old woman. "Only the games you teach me." To her relief, Kelly laughed, shaking her head.

A shadow fell across the room and Kelly's face grew serious. They stared silently at the box between them. "Do you miss your home country?"

An odd question, Mina thought. Syria was the past. She had moved on. "Canada is a better place than Syria. But yes, I miss it. I knew who I was there."

Kelly seemed to drift off, staring wistfully at the pumpkin.

Mina wondered if there was something Kelly missed too. "Is Canada your original home?"

The question shook Kelly from her reverie. "You know the saying 'home is where the heart is'?"

"No. But it's a beautiful thought."

"Yes, well." Kelly touched the pumpkin lightly with a finger. "Hold your loved ones dear while you still have them." She looked up into Mina's eye-screen, transferring a melancholy air Mina could feel instantly.

"You have no loved ones." Mina meant it as a question, but she knew the answer.

"Had a brother once," Kelly said. "We were orphans. Raised each other, we did. But he is gone now."

"I'm sorry." Mina waited, respectfully silent.

Together they studied the orange orb between them. "Well." Kelly picked up the box and hugged it close. "I think that's enough for today. See you next week?"

Mina reached across the table and put her hand over Kelly's. She squeezed it lightly. "I'll be here."

chapter 21

New Message

To   Angela Marshall

From   Susan Snow

Hi Angela!

Sorry for the delay in getting back to you. Attached are two smoothie recipes and one soup recipe that should keep you nourished and reasonably full on your "detox" days. I'd be remiss if I did not share a bit of wisdom on detoxing and deprivation. First of all, your body detoxes on its own every day. No science has proven that a juice cleanse or diet removes unhelpful elements better than the body can on its own. That said, variation is key to enjoying a balanced life, so if one day of "drinking your nutrition" a week helps you achieve that variation we all crave, then keep it going by all means.

Secondly, and I hope you won't find I'm overstepping here, but (as a friend and not as your weight-loss leader) you seem to be at a good weight for you, from what I can tell. Your impression that you will feel better 5 pounds lighter may be fed (pun not intended, lol) by your circumstances. Transitions are hard on everyone, and it sounds like you have undergone at least one major transition in the past year. We often find during transitions that what used to satisfy us no longer does. It's part of evolving as human beings, and I would encourage you to seek out a purpose or passion to replace whatever might be missing from your old life.

Although I enjoy crafting recipes to fulfill unhelpful cravings for members, part of the power of the recipes is change itself. With each change we learn something about ourselves. Learning about ourselves propels us toward new ideas, new passions, and new adventures. Perhaps we could get together for coffee sometime and talk through some of these concepts.

ShapeShifters is a good way to learn about unhelpful habits we may have picked up over time. I suspect you are smart enough to analyze your behavior now versus when you felt more in control, and figure out what is and is not helpful on your own, but if you need someone to bounce things off of, let me know. Even though you will likely "graduate" from

ShapeShifters soon, consider me your sounding board until you sort it out. Hope this is helpful.
Susan

P.S. Have you given any more thought to your goal weight?

🔼 Susan Snow
Hey there, Susan,

Thanks for those recipes. They sound great! Can't wait to try them.

Not sure you knew how much I love coffee. Throwing a shot of espresso in with some fruit and almond milk (with a wee bit of cocoa) will definitely help me with that 3:00 "do I need coffee, a treat, or both?" time of day! Genius!

Would love to have a coffee chat. You have me thinking, which I do better out loud than in my own head. Are you free tomorrow?

Not only did I lose my lawyer identity when I moved here, but I left behind quite a few good friends. I'm quickly learning that life-long friendships are not easily replaced. And yes I am thinking about the goal weight challenge you gave me and I hope to have an answer for you at the next meeting. See you soon,
Angela

P.S. Have you ever thought about making a cookbook of your recipes? Another untapped market, I think!

🔼 Angela Marshall
Angela,

Hm, now you have ME thinking too. How about CoffEEmersion on Main tomorrow at 3:00? I'll be there anyway, working on my meeting prep. Hope to see you then! Susan

Two Days Later:

Susan,

Great to see you today, and thanks for your insights on my situation. I was so blinded by gratitude for the opportunity to move to Canada and spend more time with my son, it did not cross my mind that I made two traumatic changes at once: changing careers and changing countries. Of course these life choices would come with costs as well as benefits! Much to think about!

Your manager sounds like a real tool, if you don't mind my saying. I've looked through those ShapeShifter cookbooks while waiting to weigh in and YAWN! What they really need is a cookbook designed by a leader for the members based on experience and results. He is blind to overlook that nugget of gold.

What if you gathered all those recipes together and gave them to me to distribute at the meetings? That way, all the members could benefit and it won't be coming from you 'officially.' Although, if I were you, I'd publish it outside of the company. That way you would get the credit and the proceeds.

I'm sorry to hear about your daughter's troubles at school. I think teenage years are a real struggle. My son is definitely going through something, although I'm not sure what.

Wishing you luck with the principal tomorrow,
Angela

🔺 Angela Marshall
Angela,

Sounds like we've both inspired some self-reflection in each other. I admit I like your cookbook idea. What do you think of this title? "It's Not Complicated."

I didn't know you have a teenage son. Where does he go to school?

See you soon,
Susan

🔺 Susan Marshall

Susan,
It's Not Complicated. Genius! Sign me up for one. :)
Angela

P.S. My son, Jeremy, goes to Mt. Pleasant High School.

chapter 22

THE PRINCIPAL, MRS. DERBY, STOOD IN THE OPEN DOOR OF HER OFFICE. "Come in, please," she said.

Susan and Ester swallowed hard and sprung out of their creaky lobby chairs. They nodded solemnly at the serious-faced woman in sensible shoes as they filed past her. There were five chairs in the room, all orange, seemingly leftover from the '70s. Mrs. Derby sat behind a heavy antique desk and moved a stack of files aside, smiling politely. "Thank you for coming in today."

Susan didn't wait for an intro. "Yes, I'm sure there is some misunderstanding here. Ester says she was having a private conversation with her friends, and some boy thinks he overheard a … negative comment about some other person?"

Mrs. Derby blinked.

"Sounds like a lot of 'he said, she said' with no injured party."

Mrs. Derby reviewed some notes on the computer screen beside her desk. She cleared her throat and fingered the chunky fake pearls around her neck. "The boy is rather insistent he witnessed ill will in Ester's comments. Ordinarily, we wouldn't react so quickly, but if what he said is true, we need to send a clear message."

"What did he say, exactly?" Susan gripped the side of her chair like it might tip over.

Mrs. Derby glanced at Ester, who was fidgeting with the ruffles on the hem of her blouse.

Susan had asked Ester to look presentable, rejecting the yoga pants and sweatshirt she'd worn first. But the ruffled blouse she wore now made her itchy. Susan placed a hand on her knee. "Eye contact, Ester?"

"Ester, do you have an answer to that question?" Mrs. Derby interjected.

Ester reluctantly met the principal's eyes. Then a darkness crossed her face. "How would I know what the boy thought he heard?"

The principal widened her eyes at Susan.

Susan's deadpan expression implied she had the same question.

"Perhaps you could tell us what you and your friends

were talking about, then," Mrs. Derby said. "It was about the wearing of burqas or hijabs, I believe?"

Ester shifted in her seat, folding her hands in her lap. "We were having a discussion." Ester glared upwards, studying the ceiling tiles a moment. "On whether the Muslim religion dictates that women cover themselves. You know, like in a burqa. Or whether the women have a right to choose how they dress. You know, religion-wise."

"Well," Susan said, her mind suddenly snagging on an image of Mina, running in her burqa, tripping, the viral video with the negative implications. "That sounds like a healthy academic debate to me. I don't see how questioning the limits of another culture or religion qualifies as a racial slur?"

Mrs. Derby reviewed her computer notes again. "Says here," she read, "Ester was asserting, with a loud voice others could hear in the hallway, that 'The Quran doesn't require burqas. Men require burqas to control women.'" She stopped reading to assess the impact on Susan and Ester.

Susan stared at Mrs. Derby, non-plussed. "I'm sorry. Where is the racial slur in that?"

Mrs. Derby huffed and changed her tone, like she was explaining the moon and stars to a five-year-old. "If Ester said this and in a voice loud enough for others to hear, someone who is Muslim might take offense."

Susan couldn't remember anything from the years she taught that approached this type of absurdity. "Have the rules changed since I was a teacher?" she asked with sincerity. "Did Ester attack someone directly with harsh words or fists? Because I didn't think speech qualified as an expellable offense."

Mrs. Derby touched her temple gingerly. Then she picked up the phone. "Please find young Mr. Marshall and have him come to my office." She hung up then addressed Susan. "Perhaps we should hear this from the boy himself. He was quite upset on the girl's behalf—the girl whom he thinks Ester offended. I didn't want to cause him more distress, but it seems there's no other way."

"What about the girl?" Susan said. "Shouldn't we talk to her, too? Find out what Ester's academic debate among her friends had to do with her?"

"If it comes to that," Mrs. Derby said, stroking her necklace like a pet. "The school has some liability concerns. It is best to address the matter without heightening the girl's insecurity, if possible. This is a school where diverse religions and cultures are valued. We are proud of our multicultural student body." She looked as if she might say more, then closed her mouth and gave a little nod.

The three of them waited in silence. Finally, there was a knock on the door and Mrs. Derby jumped up to let in an affable fellow with serious brown eyes. Introductions were made and the boy shook Susan's hand. He held out his hand to Ester but she cut him off by raising her palm, saying a curt "Hi."

Mrs. Derby brought around another orange chair and Jeremy sank into it, stretching his long, lanky legs to the desk's edge. "I am sorry to pull you from your classes, Mr. Marshall. What are you missing?"

"Computer science."

"Well, we will let you get back to it as soon as we can, and of course I will speak to the teacher about catching you up on what you missed." Mrs. Derby penned herself a memo as she spoke.

"It's fine," the boy said.

Susan couldn't help but notice his impossibly long lashes. They created an impression of vulnerability next to his heavy eyebrows.

"Okay then. Ester and Mrs. Snow are here to discuss the reasons Ester is being suspended. I have tried to relate the facts as you described when we met before. Some clarification is needed. Would you mind giving your account of what happened?"

"I'd rather not. You said if I put it in writing I wouldn't have to talk about it again."

Mrs. Derby smiled sympathetically. "I said I would try to avoid bringing you into this any further. But I'm sure you can understand Ester and Mrs. Snow would benefit greatly from your side of the story."

"*Story* being the key word," Susan said. "I'm sure there is more than one side to this."

The comment seemed to embolden Jeremy, who straightened in his chair. "Right," he began. "Well, what I heard can be verified by at least four or five others who were in range. Ester was practically screaming."

"Yes, I mentioned the loud voice part," Mrs. Derby said. "Can you tell us exactly what happened?"

"Sure. I was on my way to soccer tryouts. We were

meeting in the gym. And field hockey tryouts were just ending. I saw Laila. She's a new girl in our class from Syria or something like that. She's in my French class. I saw her rushing away from the gym, all upset."

"How do you know she was upset?" Ester asked. "She was wearing a hijab, which completely covered her face."

"I know because she was tearing off her head scarves … or whatever you call it … as she ran. She was crying. And running."

Ester huffed and fiddled with her ruffles.

"Anyway, I wondered why she was so upset, and then I heard Ester and some of her friends talking loudly as they were leaving the gym a few seconds later. Ester was saying that girls in burqas shouldn't be allowed to try out. And that wearing one in a civilized country is a slap in the face to women's rights."

Susan jumped in here. "Yes, we heard a bit of that, but surely Ester is allowed to debate women's rights and burqas in an academic setting."

He glared at Susan. "Maybe. But if she made Laila feel unwelcome in tryouts because of her cultural dress, that's wrong."

Ester looked up from her ruffles. "Why do you care so much?" she accused. "Do you prefer your women covered up too?"

He laughed and raised his eyebrows at Mrs. Derby.

Mrs. Derby's mouth hung open.

"Laila's nice," Jeremy finally said. "And because of you, she hasn't worn a burqa since."

The room fell silent. Susan noticed she was gritting her teeth and forced herself to breathe. *Relax.* She glanced at Ester, who shrugged her shoulders. The principal studied the carvings in her desk.

As the school bell rang, Susan considered her options. She was inclined to conclude out loud that nothing could be done until someone spoke with Laila. There was no clear connection between Ester's conduct and the girl fleeing from the gym. Then again, Susan suspected Ester was not being entirely honest about what transpired in the moments before Laila's departure. She considered asking Ester right there in the principal's office, "What did you say to that girl to upset her?" but that would have been accusatory and would likely have driven Ester further into silence.

Fortunately for Susan, Mrs. Derby spoke first. "Perhaps it is time I speak with Laila. You are all free to go for now. Ester, I'm afraid, must stay home until we understand the matter more fully."

"What?" Ester said. "That's so unfair. I'm missing team practices and class lectures because of"—she glanced over at Susan—"an academic debate with my friends?"

No one said anything, so she directed the question to her mother. "Are you going to let them get away with this?"

Susan sighed. "I think we all have some thinking and fact-finding to do." Gathering up her coat and purse, she said goodbye and exited, leaving Ester no choice but to follow.

chapter 23

ANGELA ARRIVED AT SHAPESHIFTERS HEAVY-HEARTED. Although the "detox" formula Susan gave her worked, she blew it when Jeremy seemed more out of sorts than usual. He had attacked his cereal with such ferocity, Angela wanted to intervene on the tender flakes' behalf. He gave her one-word, grunt-like answers when she inquired into his behavior. And when she asked if all was well at school, he dumped his bowl in the dishwasher with a clatter and stomped down the stairs. Angela threatened to call the school to make sure he was settling in okay, and received a thundering slam of the front door in response. She was so frustrated, she opened every cabinet in the kitchen in search of chocolate. Finding none, she had remembered the milk chocolate chips she bought for baking and polished off the whole package.

She also couldn't shake her concern about Mina. She hoped her head was okay. She scanned the meeting room, hoping for an update from Jo. But before she could recognize anyone, Angela detected trouble.

Susan was at the front desk attending to the short line of members gathered there. Behind her stood a man. That was disconcerting enough. Apart from Mina's husband on the first day, nary a male had entered the pink and chartreuse haven.

More troubling, however, was the effect this particular man seemed to have on Susan. And on the members. Instead of the cacophony of girl chat that usually greeted Angela inside those doors, it was quiet.

She watched as, one by one, each member silently stepped onto the scale, received a whispered and sedate note of encouragement from Susan, and collected a sticker before dawdling over to the meeting room.

Taking her place at the end of the line, Angela made eye contact with the man, who smiled broadly. He was dizzyingly handsome. Short cropped hair framed an angular shaven face. He wore a window-pane plaid suit with a spicy pomegranate tie that matched the room's chairs. Angela returned his smile, hoping he didn't see her lip twitch. He released his grin so quickly, Angela wondered if she'd imagined it.

He observed Susan's routine intensely, murmuring in

her ear from time to time between members. Susan nodded at each remark he made and seemed to sort the member records with less finesse than usual each time.

At last, it was Angela's turn. She avoided eye contact with the man and greeted Susan. Susan smiled professionally and invited Angela onto the scale, under the red-hot glare of the hyper-observant man.

"You seem to have a growth," Angela said.

Susan's chin jerked up. "Sorry?"

"There's a man attached to your hip." Angela tried to smile nicely at the hip growth.

Susan shot the man a look and laughed nervously. "This is Angela, one of our newest members."

He said, "Oh, hello, how are you?" in such a way that revealed no interest in an answer.

"Angela, this is Marty McGomery. He is visiting today. He's our territory manager and he will be observing the meeting." She said all this in a voice full of fake cheer.

"Great," Angela said without meaning it. "Listen, I blew it this morning. Jeremy was all out of sorts, and I basically inhaled all the chocolate I could find in the kitchen after he went to school."

Susan smiled sympathetically and jotted down Angela's weight in the record book. "Well," she said, "That takes care of the 'what didn't go so well for you this week' question." She handed Angela a sticker that said, 'Rainbows come with rain,' and placed her weight record on the bottom of a shaky stack.

"Thanks," Angela said, stepping off the scale.

"Have you given any thought to a goal weight?" Marty McMuffin, or whatever his name was, said.

Angela froze abruptly as if shot in the back. Recovering, she replied icily, "Yes, I will be happy to discuss the topic of my weight goal with Susan." She turned to leave, then added, "Privately," before hurrying off to the meeting room.

The nerve, she thought as she sauntered step after irritable step to the meeting room. She wondered if this happened often—the manager showing up and grilling members who were only at ease stepping on to a scale because of Susan's inviting demeanor. She considered writing a scathing letter to the company, detailing the extent of her embarrassment from interrogation by a talking head from some out-of-touch administrative office. Before she got too far in her thinking, she realized that would only reflect poorly on Susan and she best leave ShapeShifters business to ShapeShifters employees.

She scanned the room, relieved to find Mina in the back row, chatting it up with Jo. Angela sat by Jo. "Thank God you're here," she said to Mina. "I've been worried about you. Hi, Jo."

Jo looked at her with a friendly furrowed brow. "Damn right," she said. "I told her I'd hunt her down if I didn't see her at the meeting."

Mina's melodic giggles melted some tension from the weigh-in. "I'm fine," she said. "The swelling went down days ago. You can barely see the bump. It's just a little scratch."

She turned her head to her lap and added, "Sorry to worry you."

"No worries at all." Angela touched Mina's arm. "Just glad you're okay."

Susan began the meeting unremarkably, noting that Halloween was coming. She had members add their favorite ghoul-ish treats to a list she plotted out on the whiteboard in orange and black markers.

Marty McLurker took a seat in the back, on the other side of the room from Angela and her pals. After the list was complete, Susan started asking for strategies to avoid over-doing it when candy showed up at the office or when kids dumped pillowcases of chocolate on kitchen tables.

Manager-Man listened and jotted down occasional notes in a leather-bound notepad.

The members seemed more hesitant than usual to cop to their mistakes. Angela could still taste the velvety goodness of the chocolate chips she inhaled hours before.

When one of the seasoned members mentioned how she wasn't even tempted by Halloween candy anymore since she got her hands on the Crave-Killer Cookie recipe, a shadow seemed to fall across Susan's face. She glanced at Manager-Man, who was fiercely scribbling away. Then she scrawled "find a more filling alternative" on the solutions side of the "tempting treats" list and immediately asked who else had some good strategies.

Jo elbowed Angela. "That sounds like gold," she whispered. Then to the seasoned member who mentioned the recipe, she stage-whispered, "Hey! Can I get that recipe from you?"

Before Susan could react, the woman enthusiastically

nodded. "Of course! They are so filling. Chocolate but also peanut butter and oats so they satisfy the craving while filling me up. They're great."

She turned to Susan. "I got the recipe from you, though. Maybe you can print some off for the new members?"

Again with the pin-drop silence. Susan gaped helplessly in the manager's direction like a stunned animal. Marty McSomething sat glaring at the carpet. A few members turned to one another to see if maybe they missed something.

Finally, Susan said quietly, "That's a good suggestion, Martha. We certainly encourage members to share their recipes. Unfortunately, I can no longer provide my own recipes for you." Then she put on a fake happy face. "But talk to me after the meeting and I will point out which tasty products on the sale-wall help the most with chocolate cravings. Why, I believe the Polka Mocha Smoothies are on sale this week!"

Jo turned to Angela and mouthed "What. The. Fuck?"

Angela shrugged and checked out the manager's reaction. He was nodding sternly but approvingly.

Unfortunately for Susan, the topic didn't end there. One member asked why she couldn't share her recipes anymore. Another member mentioned the Simply Filling Soup recipe she got from Susan and wanted to know if there was something wrong with it. Two women in the front row got up and moved next to Martha in the third row, pulling out their phones to exchange contact information. Martha assured them she could scan and email the recipe when she got home. Overhearing this, more members crowded around Martha, and the din was so loud, Susan had to turn the lights on and off to get them focused back on her. She concluded the meeting quickly and made a beeline for the front desk where she busied herself with paperwork rather than mingling with members like she usually did.

Angela lingered a moment in the lobby, feeling a bit lost and wanting the Crave-Killer Cookie recipe herself. While she waited for the crowd around Martha to thin, she inspected the products on the sale-shelf. She picked up the Polka Mocha Smoothie box and checked out the ingredients. There were no vegetables or fruits in it. It was some kind of powder mix, so she put the box back. Belinda sidled up next to her and asked if she was going to try it.

"No," Angela said. "Susan gave me a couple of amazing smoothie recipes this week. They don't have weird chemicals in them. I can bring a copy to our next training run if you'd like?" She didn't hear Belinda's response because at that moment she saw Manager-Man a few steps behind, glaring at the two of them. She stared back blankly, gathering the impression she had mis-stepped. He turned around slowly and walked behind the front desk where Susan was shuffling paperwork.

As Angela drew closer, she heard him ask Susan, "Is it true you sent your own recipes to a member this week? After I told you to stop?"

Susan's eyes slowly rose up to catch Angela's. "Yes," she admitted quietly. "But—"

"You're fired," he said.

24

LAILA WORKED HARD AT INVISIBILITY. She sat at the back of class. She let her chemistry lab partners take the lead. And she prepared carefully for French, uttering concise phrases when asked. Never elaborating. Other students blended like ghosts, but she had achieved maximum ghost-ness.

It had been two weeks since she ditched the burqa. A few students did a double-take the first day she came to school without it. But the whispered rumors about the field hockey episode faded quickly. The Grade 10 girl who might be pregnant and the Grade 11 boy whose life might be ruined shifted to the limelight. And just like that, Laila reclaimed invisibility.

Being invisible with a burqa felt different than being invisible without one. People cared that you wore a burqa but mostly pretended they didn't. When you didn't wear one, they had nothing to care about. The issue was removed from notice like a word deleted from a screen.

But all her progress was now in jeopardy. She was so used to wandering Mount Pleasant High School's hallways worry-free that she didn't see it coming. When Mrs. Derby set her heart thudding so hard she felt each beat like a baseball bat to the neck, she found herself caught in the cross-hairs once again.

"Someone has complained on your behalf about an unfortunate occurrence," Mrs. Derby had begun. But Laila was smart. By the time she left the office, Mrs. Derby knew less than before.

To make sure, though, she had to do one more thing. She paced outside French class, waiting for the boy who complained. She intended to remove the incident from history. To maintain her invisibility, she checked Instagram while waiting, peering over her phone every ten seconds to scan for Jeremy.

Myra, a friend of Ester's, had posted a picture of the field hockey team. "Voted team captain," the caption said. "#humbled." Laila made sure she liked all the photos of the students she followed. It sealed her invisibility. People noticed when you didn't like or comment. She commented, "Congratulations!" with star, thumbs-up, and girl-with-hockey-stick emojis. She wondered why Ester wasn't in the team shot and secretly savored the fantasy of her failing to win the team captain votes. Then she chided herself. Only a bad person would feel happy about someone's misfortune. *But maybe Ester didn't want to be captain*, she thought consolingly.

Jeremy appeared around the corner two minutes before the bell. Students jammed the hallway, grabbing supplies from lockers, walking in pairs and small groups, breaking into sprints at the one-minute mark.

She walked toward Jeremy cautiously, making sure no one was watching.

He saw her instantly. The way his eyes connected with hers, the red tint that crept up his neck, made her uneasy. But she made up her mind to put an end to what he started.

"Can I talk to you?" She waited until he was close enough to hear her gentle but confident voice.

His eyes widened. He stopped and slouched a little. He was taller than she realized. "Sure," he said, like a question.

She looked around quickly. One or two people glanced her way as they streaked past. She needed to do this fast. Before it became a thing. "I know you filed a complaint. About something that's none of your business. Withdraw it," she said. "Please."

The bell rang and she turned her back to Jeremy, drawing up her invisibility cloak, but Jeremy caught her elbow and whipped her back around. He towered over her, her arm locked tight in his grasp. But his eyes were kind. For a moment she was lost in their softness. "Why?" he said.

They were almost alone in the hallway now; the last few students ogled them as they dashed by. Laila started to panic. People who walked in late were the opposite of invisible. "Please," she said. "Let me go." The grip on Laila's arm stayed firm. Jeremy's chocolate eyes searched hers for answers with no sign of relenting, so she added, "I'll … I'll explain after class."

He raised an eyebrow.

"I promise," she said.

Finally, he released her arm. She bolted the last few feet to the classroom door. All the students were either in their seats or almost there, and Laila felt eyes on her that grew more intense as Jeremy trailed inches behind her.

"Vite, vite!" the teacher was saying, plus something about "*retard*" and "*inacceptable*." Laila and Jeremy took the first chairs they could find, which ended up being across from each other.

"*Je suis désolé*," Jeremy said, attracting more incoherent reprimands from the teacher.

After what felt like hours, the French tirade wound its way to explanatory teaching. Mme. Blanche turned toward the blackboard and wrote out a French sentence for discussion.

Laila took out her laptop and opened her French Notes file. She selected a new document, dated it, and copied down the sentence on the board. As Mme. Blanche fired questions at the class, she typed them into Google Translate and tried to keep up. A Facebook message popped up in the corner of her screen. It was from Jeremy. She looked over at him, but he was staring straight ahead, Google Translate open on his laptop as well. Laila clicked on the message.

"Why won't you stand up to her?" it said.

Laila replied, "I am here to learn, not cause trouble."

"It won't matter if I withdraw the complaint," he said.

"Yes it will. If no one is complaining, no one gets in trouble."

"She's already suspended," he wrote.

Laila stared at the words in disbelief. She thought about the team photo with Ester missing and Myra taking Ester's usual role of team captain. A family of butterflies batted about in Laila's stomach. For a few seconds she couldn't breathe.

Jeremy wrote again. "You didn't know. I'm sorry."

Laila ignored this and turned her attention to Mme. Blanche. She couldn't think about this now. She had to stay focused.

Another message appeared. "What did she say to you that day?"

When the bell rang, Laila grabbed her laptop and shoved it into her backpack, leaving the class as quickly as possible. She could feel the walls closing in on her. Ester would be angry about missing school. She would be angry about not being team captain. What if she missed being on the team altogether? Laila would have a target on her back over this.

She power-walked to her locker downstairs and considered her options. She could go back to wearing the burqa. Would that put an end to this? She didn't want to go back, though. It was too much work, it was too limiting, too much of an attention-magnet.

Maybe this would blow over. The principal needed her side of the story to pin anything on Ester. She would be allowed back, the suspension revoked. It might still be okay. She heard steps behind her as Jeremy caught up, walking alongside her as she made her way down the hall.

"You said you'd explain after class," he said.

Laila stopped, exasperated. "Why do you care so much?"

He looked at his shoes, then at her, opening his mouth to speak. Then stared at his shoes some more.

Laila waited for an answer.

"The thing is," he finally said, "I saw you running out of the gym that day." His chocolate eyes locked onto Laila's and melted the invisible border she carefully built around herself. "And I thought you were beautiful."

Laila felt a wave of something she didn't recognize. Her fingertips tingled. Her heart skipped a beat. Her head felt so light it almost floated. She couldn't find words, so she just stared back at him like an idiot.

"All I knew was that I had to do something about whatever it was that caused you pain."

The bell rang and Laila realized how far from class she was. She should have been panicked but all she felt at that moment was a fierce desire to stay exactly where she was, looking up into the eyes of this person who bared his heart to her.

Jeremy seemed to recognize her reluctance to move. He started walking and she fell into step beside him. As they walked, he said, "Listen, if you tell me what Ester said to you, I'll talk to Mrs. Derby about letting this go."

chapter 25

SUSAN DIDN'T NOTICE LEX TALKING TO HER, AND SHE DIDN'T KNOW HOW LONG SHE'D BEEN IN HER HOUSECOAT.

"Are you going to work today?" Lex eyed his wife over the bar, where he stood sampling her latest creations. Pumpkin oat scones with maple frosting this time. He had never seen Susan lounge on the sofa, let alone with her feet on the armrests. "Did you hear me?"

Susan flinched. "What?" Suddenly conscious of the dreamy tone in her voice, she straightened a little and pushed her mouth into a smile. Perhaps this was why she had never watched TV in the daytime. It was addictive. And mind-altering.

"Isn't this the day you work?"

Susan heard the question over what felt like an expanse of water. Work. Hmmm. Missing work would be a temporary thing. She knew Marty would call any day now and apologize, admit he was wrong, give her the promotion she deserved. Best not to trouble Lex with such minor issues. "Oh yes," she said. "I'm just …"

"These scones are your best yet, babe." Lex brightened, opting to cheer her with compliments. His eyes glazed over with pleasure as he chewed. "So light and moist. And the maple!" He gave her two thumbs up after he shoved the last morsel into his mouth. "Mmm!"

Susan tried her best to break the TV trance. She tucked her knees into her chest and straightened some more, almost knocking the open bag of chips off her lap. "That's nice, sweetie," she managed. "Can you tell which ones are gluten-free?"

His face darkened in contemplation as he examined her more closely. She saw his eyes move from her housecoat and crumbs on her collar, which she brushed off absentmindedly, to the daytime drama taking place on TV. "Uh, the ones on the left? You okay?"

"Hm? Oh. Yep." Susan made a show of closing the bag of chips. She looked around for the chip-clip. "Next baking project, I'm going to make chips like this I think," she said.

Lex crossed the room to pick up the bag. "No-Name Ruffles? All Dressed?"

"Right." Susan cleared her throat, trying to find another subject. Her phone rang in the kitchen. She ignored it, entranced again by the handsome actor on TV who'd been lying to his wife.

Lex took the chip bag to the kitchen. "It's from the school," he shouted, then answered her phone.

Susan raised a hand to her mouth but there was no chip in it.

Lex came over to the couch with her phone. "The principal is asking if today at one works for you and Ester to come in."

"Sure thing. Tell her that's fine." *Something about those eyes*, Susan thought, still watching the TV couple dance around his obvious cheating. *That's how he gets away with those lies.*

Lex confirmed with the principal, set the phone down, and turned his attention back to Susan. "Did you resolve the suspension issue?" He sat down on an ottoman across from his wife, blocking her view of the TV.

Susan gave her head a shake, taking the clicker off her lap and turning the TV off. "Not yet. That's what this meeting is for, I think. Mrs. Derby had to talk to the girl whom Ester supposedly offended. How weird is it that she didn't do that from the start?"

"Very weird. Remind her what a stellar student she is, will you? This won't hurt her university applications, I hope."

Susan nodded, then shook her head.

"Maybe I should come with you." Lex's eyebrows

furrowed in concern. "I can get someone to cover for me at work."

"You can if you like," Susan said without conviction. "I'm sure it will be fine either way." *I am a good mother*, Susan reminded herself. *I am a good weight-loss leader.* Children of good mothers didn't get suspended. Good leaders didn't get fired.

"Alright then." Lex kissed her on the forehead. "You sure you're okay?"

Susan tried to sound reassuring. "I'm good." She smiled so wide her cheeks hurt.

***

"Mom. MOM!"

Susan jolted awake. She propped herself up on one elbow and brushed a few crumbs from her face. Ester stood over her. She wore her white funeral blouse with a classic black skirt.

"Wow, you look …" Susan rarely saw Ester out of her athletic wear twice in one week. When did she start looking so mature?

"Mom! Aren't we supposed to be at the principal's at one?"

Susan searched her mind. Lex, the scones, her phone ringing. "Oh. Oh. What time is it?"

"Ten to." Ester's eyes assessed the situation scornfully: the couch, her mother's unpolished state, the droning TV.

Susan jumped off the couch, ran out into the foyer, and rummaged around in the closet for her best fall boots.

"Mom."

Ester was behind her, hands on hips, her expression a mix between startled and disappointed. Ester looked her mother up and down, expression unreadable. Susan saw her own bare feet with chipped toenail polish, her white housecoat dripping bits of crumbs onto the marble floor. She felt her eyes widen at Ester, silently pleading for answers. How could she be late for something this important? Why did she feel so unmotivated? Ester's expression softened a minute amount.

"I'll grab some clothes," Ester said. She frowned at her mother. "Gather yourself, okay?"

Susan nodded as Ester flew up the stairs. She was still nodding when Ester came down with a couple of Susan's go-to presentable-in-most-scenarios outfits. She chose the black skinny jeans with a loose white top. Ester handed her the taupe bra while Susan stripped off her robe shamelessly. Finally, she zipped up her black dress boots and Ester handed her the ruffled gray sweater on their way out the door. The car was locked. Ester held out the keys and said, "I'll drive."

"Right." Susan checked her shoulder for the purse that wasn't there. She sauntered over to the passenger side, her mind already slipping into co-pilot mode.

Ester launched into the parental-type monologue Susan might have given as she drove. "So whatever the principal says, just agree," Ester warned. "I'll speak if something needs to be said."

Susan nodded, noticing how the buildings blurred when she relaxed her eyes.

"We should be prepared for worst case," Ester continued.

"Laila and her parents. Jeremy and his parents. They may all be there. And the principal."

Susan nodded and wondered if they had time to stop for donuts.

"Are you listening, Mother?"

She looked at Ester. "Yes. Yes, I am." She tried to focus.

"So worst case, Laila comes up with something I may have said that spurred her to do the scarf ripping-off drama, Jeremy backs her up, I get my suspension affirmed, and I'm screwed for university."

Susan let this sink in, her focus narrowing in on the last words. "Screwed for university … Oh, God."

"Exactly," Ester said. "Do you have my back, Mom? Or not?"

Susan looked over at her nearly-grown daughter, driving the two of them to a meeting that could affect Ester's future. "What *did* you say to Laila?"

Ester didn't answer right away. After she slid into a parking space and turned off the car, she sighed. "I thought I was being helpful. She's pretty good at field hockey. I mean, really good." She looked at Susan to see if this registered. "She was tireless, running up and down the field ahead of the others, even after we ran the drills like ten times. She had mid-fielder written all over her."

She opened her backpack and dropped the keys inside. Then she sat back, staring out the car window like she was watching the practice all over again. Shaking her head slowly, Ester frowned. "Only problem was she couldn't see the ball. She'd be perfectly positioned. And I'd try to pass to her, but ... It was so frustrating! So I said something like 'You'd really be something without the ghost outfit.'"

Susan blinked, waiting for Ester to say, "Just kidding, I wouldn't say something that crass," but she didn't. She just stared at her hands folded in her lap.

"You really said 'ghost outfit'?"

"Yyyep. To be fair, though, I didn't know what to call it until I was talking to my friends about it after. There are so many words for those coverings. Burqa, hijab, niqab ... I can't keep it straight."

Wordlessly, Susan and Ester opened their car doors, then walked up the steps and through the main entrance doors.

chapter 26

ANGELA HAD TO ADMIT, SHE PRETENDED SHE HADN'T HEARD MARTY SAY THE WORDS "YOU'RE FIRED" TO SUSAN AT THE END OF THE LAST MEETING. Just as the words were spoken, the Crave-Killer Cookie recipe lady walked past her to leave. Angela had been waiting for the crowd around her to thin, so she stopped Martha just outside the ShapeShifters doors and set up a contact exchange so she could get her hands on that recipe.

She ended up talking to Martha for so long, and after that with Mina, who was not as well versed with her cell phone, that by the time she promised Mina a paper copy of the recipe and said her goodbyes to Jo and Belinda, the ShapeShifter doors were closed and locked. She drove home, fixated on making the recipe before entering a grocery filled with Oreos and Fritos.

It wasn't until now, hanging up her puffy coat in the ShapeShifters lobby a week later, that it occurred to her the words she repressed had actually been spoken. That this meeting, this little haven of honesty and acceptance, this enclave of truth-in-weighing, had changed forever. There was something wrong. Two things, in fact.

The first wrong thing was Marty, with his plastic smile, standing at the counter, towering above everyone with his over-confidence. The second wrong thing was the woman next to him. She was basically Susan's opposite. Whereas Susan's radiant skin, golden hair, and self-assured demeanor were a beacon to all who wanted to better themselves, this woman had wrinkles, red splotches in front of her ears, and bristly hair that bent unnaturally toward a forehead that extended too far from her narrow eyes. Her shoulders were wide and lumpy, suggesting a less-than-fit frame. And when she looked up, prompted by Marty's elbow, her expression was one of agitation rather than warmth.

"Good morning," Marty enthused, offering no explanation for wrong thing #1 and wrong thing #2.

"Morning?" Angela felt weak, searching in vain for any option other than weighing in with these two characters. Although nothing else was amiss in the meeting room, she had the impression of wrongness imprinting itself on the entire experience yet to come. She dragged herself to the counter and numbly performed the routine of setting down her purse, taking off her shoes, and dumping her clunky watch on the counter. "I'm Angela," she managed to say to wrong thing #2, avoiding eye contact as much as possible with wrong thing #1.

"Of course, Angela, great to see you again," Marty said, unconvincingly. "This is Magdala."

"You can call me Madge," wrong thing #2 said, extending a pudgy hand for shaking.

Shaking Madge's hand was like handling a dirty dishrag. Angela cringed, then stepped on the scale. Marty showed Madge how to record the weight and assemble the cards so statistics could be easily discerned by the end of the meeting. He handed Angela a sticker. It was a graduation hat with 'Congrats' written on it.

"What's this mean?" Angela became aware of the tiny hairs on the back of her neck. Unease grew into anger one hair at a time.

"You are at your ideal weight," Marty said. "We will celebrate in the meeting. Congrats." The plastic smile did not waver. His mechanical voice stoked a fire in Angela's stomach.

"By whose estimation am I at my ideal weight?" she asked acidly.

Madge looked at the card again, then at Marty for help.

Marty sighed. "It's a ShapeShifters estimation." He took the card from Madge and placed it in the stack. "There are health-based rules that govern the appropriate BMI weight for your height. And age."

Angela saw his lips moving and failed to appreciate the sounds they made.

Marty shifted his weight to one foot. Then another. He made eye contact with the next person in line. "Hi there," he said to Belinda. "Congrats again," he said to Angela as a send off.

Angela turned to greet Belinda, who showed no sign of moving up in line. "Did you make your goal weight?" Belinda asked.

"Hard to make a goal weight before coming up with a goal," Angela said.

"Oh." Belinda took a step back. "That's weird. Does ShapeShifters set the goal weight, or does the member? I don't know how it works."

"The member," Jo said from behind Belinda. "This isn't my first rodeo." She winked at Angela. "My first time here, it took me months to get to a place where I could imagine a goal. Then it took another three months to reach my goal. I still have my Goal Diploma." She beamed with pride as she said it.

The line behind Jo was out the door now, and Marty was getting antsy. "That's not always how—"

"Here you go." Angela placed the grad hat sticker on the counter. "When I'm ready to set my goal weight, I'll let you …" She tried to imagine announcing her goal to either Marty or Madge. "Well, I will be the one to set it. Thank you." She turned around and gestured to Belinda. "Your turn, my friend." Then to Jo: "Thanks, Jo."

Denial was definitely not working for Angela now.

Not only was Susan missing unceremoniously from the meeting, but her replacements were trying to bully Angela into concluding her journey at ShapeShifters. She marched into the meeting room and, being first to arrive and also responsible for holding up the line, sat in the first row. Taking out her phone, she emailed Susan.

Susan,

Where are you? Two inauthentic aliens have taken over your place at the meeting. Please advise.

Angela

P.S. It's all wrong here without you.
P.S.S. I miss you.

She clicked send and saw she had a message in her now-refreshed inbox. It was from the school.

Mr. and Mrs. Marshall:

There will be a meeting in my office today at 1:00 p.m. on a matter that concerns your son. You are invited to attend, but not required. I apologize for the late notice, but a prompt resolution of the matter is my priority. Hope to see you there,

Mrs. Penelope Derby

Angela texted Jeremy: "Do you know what the meeting in your principal's office is about?"

She refreshed the email screen. No new messages. She checked her texts. Her message to Jeremy had been delivered but not read.

Mina sat down beside her. "What's wrong?"

Angela frowned at her phone. "Oh, hi, Mina." She refreshed again. Nothing. "How was your weigh-in?"

"Better." Mina's voice betrayed a bright smile. "Those cookies were such a help. I didn't realize how many sugary snacks pass my lips when I'm at home. One cookie with my tea was all I needed, it turns out."

"They are excellent. I agree." Angela continued to frown at her phone without elaborating.

Mina patted Angela's knee. "You upset about Susan?"

"Yes!" Angela had almost forgotten. "It's all wrong." She glanced again at her phone as Mina nodded in agreement. "I'm sorry to be distracted, Mina. I've been called into my son's school for a meeting with the principal, and I'm not sure why."

"Me too!" Mina sounded breathless. "I saw the email before I left this morning. Mine is at one. How about you?"

Angela stared into Mina's eye-screen incredulously. "Same. Where did you say Laila goes to school?"

And to Angela's utmost surprise, Mina said, "Mount Pleasant."

chapter

27

JEREMY WAS ON HIS WAY TO HIS LOCKER TO GRAB LUNCH WHEN HE SAW HIS MOTHER'S TEXT. *Oh fuck. Shit just got real.* He changed course, making a beeline downstairs toward Laila's locker. He wouldn't see her in French until after lunch. Too late to warn her. He had never seen her between classes, but he made a silent prayer to everything holy that he would find her somehow.

The last time he saw her, he suspected she liked him too. But then he pushed too hard about Ester, and an invisible screen seemed to close around her, shutting him out. If he could just find her, apologize, let her know he was on her side, this meeting might not be as painful as he imagined. She wasn't at her locker. He lingered there a few minutes, hoping.

His phone vibrated. Another text from Mom. "I'm on my way to the principal. Would love to know what this is about?"

Jeremy grimaced. "Don't worry. I'm not in trouble. Just a witness," he typed.

"To what?" she texted immediately.

Jeremy didn't answer. *What is the answer?* he wondered. Bullying? Insensitivity? He had seen the mean-girl thing play out many times at his old school. There did not seem to be a remedy for it. Teachers chalked it up to kids being kids. Like physical harm is the only harm deserving of punishment. In an era of metal detectors at each entrance, mental suffering was something to wait out, like a simmering pot of peppers. Only if it erupted into physical violence would school administrators get involved. Never mind if it was too late.

To be honest, Jeremy was surprised the principal at Mount Pleasant would bother with this at all. His impulse to complain was driven by a churning furnace inside him, something that chewed on his powerful attraction to Laila, the kinship he believed they shared as new students in a high school where everyone seemed to know each other from birth.

Yes, that's what rankled him the most. Laila's shedding of her customary clothes resonated. How hard would it be for him to shed the customary concepts he brought with him to a country that was chosen for him, not by him?

Jeremy's stomach growled for the peanut butter sandwich he had in his locker. As he sat by Laila's locker, small groups formed along the wall up and down the hallway—students who probably gave up, as he usually did, finding room in the crowded lunch area.

Time passed slowly. He took out his phone and sent Laila a Facebook message, wishing he had her cell number. "You coming to the 1:00 meeting?" No response and no Laila by 12:55, so he got up and ambled slowly to the main office.

Angela was standing outside the office doors, checking her phone and looking worried. A woman in a burqa stood near her. Jeremy's heart skipped a beat at first, thinking it was Laila. But this woman was shorter, and as she turned around to enter the office doors, he saw she had wider hips.

"There you are!" his mom called out when she spotted him in the crowd.

"Hi, Mom." Jeremy gave Angela a little hug to defuse whatever might be brewing within her. She smiled and seemed to forget what she was going to ask. *Perfect.* Before she could think of it, he asked, "Has Laila arrived yet? I guess that's her mother who just walked in there." He pointed to the shrouded figure behind the smoked-glass office door.

His mom brightened. "Funny story! She *is* Laila's mother, and I know her from ShapeShifters. Isn't that wild? She's one of my best friends, actually."

Jeremy appeared more concerned than appreciative of the connection. "Is she the one in the viral video?"

"What viral video?" His mom looked surprised.

"Oh, I meant to show it to you." Jeremy checked his phone. No message from Laila. "A bunch of women standing around a Muslim woman on the ground. Some of the memes are funny, but I guess it's kind of mean."

"I don't know if she's Muslim. Does a burqa necessarily equal Muslim?"

Jeremy shrugged. "Isn't it a religious practice?"

Angela just stood there, thinking.

"Anyway," Jeremy said, "all the women standing in the meme are wearing ShapeShifters T-shirts. A lot of the memes just change the T-shirts to say funny things like '#metoo' and whatever else might be trending."

"Oh, that's awful," Angela said. She looked at her watch. "Time to go in."

Jeremy walked in behind her, grateful he didn't have to tell her the whole story more than once about what they were all doing there. Once inside, he saw Laila's mom talking to Ester's mom.

"Oh my God," Angela said. "Does Ester go to this school too?" she asked Susan.

As it turned out, the three moms knew each other from ShapeShifters, which was a weird coincidence and also humiliating. He knew how women, especially mothers, talked. This incident would be a permanent part of their conversations, he predicted, assuming they would be talking to each other at all after the meeting.

Angela and Mina continued an animated discussion about their kids and the bizarre ShapeShifters meeting. Jeremy noticed

Susan was not as engaged. She stayed seated next to Ester, staring wistfully at the clock.

Finally, the principal called them in. Jeremy's mom peppered Susan with questions about where she had been and why she was fired and could she have her phone number so she could keep her advised about the ShapeShifters meetings? Susan merely nodded and walked like there was molasses under her shoes.

In Mrs. Derby's office, they sat awkwardly, crammed into the orange chairs. Mrs. Derby introduced everyone. Ester actually looked a bit stricken, like she was ready to apologize. Her mom, Susan, looked like she was wigged out on drugs. Angela was searching all the faces anxiously. She seemed perplexed. This was probably not the way she wanted to visit his new school: in the principal's office with random people she knew and no clue what she was there for.

"Where's Laila?" Jeremy asked to get the ball rolling. *The sooner we do this, the sooner we can all get on with our lives.*

Laila's mom jerked her head in Jeremy's direction. "She's not here?"

Mrs. Derby said she'd check the attendance rolls. While she did, Jeremy noticed Ester was dressed better than usual. Her severe white blouse and black skirt, and her hair pulled back in a tight ponytail, made her look younger and less confident somehow. She fixated on the hem of her skirt, pulling at a loose string. The muscle in her thigh flexed like a heartbeat.

"I'm sorry, I don't know if she's here yet," Mrs. Derby said, finally. "Her homeroom teacher hasn't turned in the attendance. I talked to her yesterday, though. She knows about the meeting." She typed something into her computer. "Perhaps we should wait a few minutes, in case she's just running late."

"She's never late," Mina said. Jeremy's mom touched her arm.

"Look, while we're waiting," Angela said, "Can someone fill me in on why we're here?" She looked over at her son. "Jeremy says he was a witness to something?"

"He overheard a private conversation," Ester said to her skirt.

"Loudest private conversation on the face of the earth," Jeremy said, his sympathy for Ester dissolving.

"Yes, well," Mrs. Derby interrupted. "The hope today was that Laila could speak for herself and fill us all in. The complaint that was made by this young man here"—she gestured to Jeremy—"relates to what might be construed as hate speech or bullying in the extreme, and insensitive at the very least. This young lady"—she pointed at Ester—"is on suspension for now until we resolve the matter."

"Well, what did she say?" Angela asked Jeremy.

"We don't know what she said to Laila exactly." Jeremy shifted slightly in his under-sized chair. "But afterwards, Laila ran out of the field hockey tryouts crying and tearing off her burqa." He looked at Laila's mom here; there was a faint gasp behind her veil. "I heard Ester saying that burqas are like a step back for womankind or something like that." Jeremy stopped to see if his words were having any impact on Ester. She shot him a little glare and went back to picking at her skirt. "I found it rather offensive."

"Well, surely Ester knows what she said," Angela speculated, eyeing Susan. Then Ester. "Did you say something to Laila before she ran out, honey?"

Ester glared at Angela. "If I did, it's a matter between me and Laila." She gestured around the room. "Since she's not here, my guess is she has no bone to pick with me or anyone else. I mean, geez, we're teenagers, aren't we? Emotional outbursts are in our DNA."

Angela's mouth hung open for a few seconds, then she closed it. Susan, sitting right next to Ester, failed to have any reaction whatsoever. She stared ahead at the colorful artwork behind Mrs. Derby's desk.

"Is that what you think too, Susan?" Angela said.

Susan blinked, turned to acknowledge Angela, and focused her gaze a bit. "Ester was trying to help, I think," she said, resuming her interest in Mrs. Derby's art wall. Ester elbowed her mother, giving her a reproachful look. Susan answered by absentmindedly patting her on the knee.

"Trying to help," Jeremy said. "Mind explaining that for us, Ester?" *This oughta be good.*

Ester bore her steely eyes into his and said, "Like I said, it's between me and Laila."

"Oh, for Pete's sake," Angela barked. "I really don't see—"

"She was probably bullied, Mom," Jeremy said. "That's when someone with power deliberately makes someone without power feel like shit."

"Language, young man," Mrs. Derby said.

"Sorry," Jeremy said to Mrs. Derby. He continued his condescending tone aimed at his mother. "Ester is a rockstar of sports around here."

"Thank you," said Ester.

"You're not welcome." This to Ester. And to his mother, "Laila is new to the school, like me. She had no power. So Ester had a duty to be a good example, maybe even mentor her, show her the fu— friggin ropes."

"Wow," Ester said. "Are you two married or something? Maybe that's why she took off her burqa."

Jeremy looked to Mrs. Derby. "See? She doesn't get it." He stared at Ester incredulously. "There are so many layers of wrong in what you just said, I don't know how to begin."

"You can begin by minding your own business," Ester said.

"Alright, that will be enough with the accusations," Mrs. Derby said, glancing at the door. "If Laila doesn't want to complain, this meeting resolves nothing. I have an idea, though." She pulled up some files on her computer. "The school board requires programming for bullying, bystander syndrome, resilience, and sensitivity for the students. Jeremy, how would you feel about working on this program with Ester? The idea is to organize a student-led presentation. On bullying in general," she added.

"What? No." Jeremy smacked his thigh. "Why do I have to be punished for sticking up for Laila?"

"That sounds like a waste of time," Ester said.

"Does suspension sound like a better use of your time?" Mrs. Derby asked Ester.

Before she could answer, there was a knock on the door. Mrs. Derby yelled, "Come in!" and in walked Laila. In her burqa.

chapter

28

EARLIER THAT DAY, LAILA HAD A VISION DURING MORNING PRAYERS: IF TAKING OFF HER BURQA EARNED HER THE UNWANTED ATTENTION SHE WAS GETTING NOW, THEN THE SOLUTION LAY IN PUTTING THE BURQA BACK ON. She kind of liked the attention she got from Jeremy. But that was another story. The main thing was to get Ester off the hook so Laila could retreat from this unwanted controversy.

As she dressed for school, she reflected on how easily she fell into the routine of skipping the noon and afternoon prayers after they moved. She knew no Muslim girls at school. Certainly no girls in burqas. She kept her eye out for observers who might excuse themselves from class at the right moments, but no one ever did. She compensated by saying the missed prayers before the Maghrib prayer each evening. It took longer, but she became more focused with each prayer, telling herself she was getting more out of the prayers by lumping them together.

She could not reconcile this knowledge with her fierce desire to be a ghost in the school. If she was called to be humble, how could God condone her making such waves for a couple of prayer times during the school day? If God had led her family to this land, as her parents insisted, why would he not also show her how to reconcile her faith with the values of this "more civilized" (her parents' words) society?

She allowed herself to believe that her faith was wrong, she realized. Her faith, which left girls no choice but to be imprisoned in their homes so as to not miss key prayer times. Her faith, that drew unwanted attention to her clothing when she was unable to participate in healthy activities like sport. She reasoned that her faith must evolve to embrace the clear opportunities of the West while keeping the essential tenants that she held dear. That was how she came to believe a short-sleeved T-shirt and jeans were an acceptable compromise to the more revealing outfits of her peers. And that saying her prayers extra well at night made up for the ones she missed while gaining the education her parents felt was so valuable.

But now. Now she had drawn attention by reacting to inane comments of an uninformed peer. Instead of rising above it, she let it get to her. And now she felt the pull of Allah directing her to a way of avoiding more unwanted attention. If she put the burqa back on, she demonstrated she had not rejected her faith. She could exercise her right to cover up or not cover up, within the bounds of common sense humility, and make the supposed offense against her fall away.

She made polite conversation with her mother over breakfast and wondered if she was in fact feeling God's direction or seeking a way out, a fearful act rather than a courageous one. When her mother left for her ShapeShifters meeting, Laila returned to her prayer rug.

When she received no further guidance, she chided herself for expecting such a blessing when it was not yet time for the next prayer. That is when it dawned on her she could stay home for the Zuhr prayer. It was her last chance to receive guidance and find some courage before the 1:00 p.m. meeting.

chapter 29

JEREMY'S HEART CAUGHT IN HIS THROAT AS LAILA APPEARED IN THE DOORWAY.

"Laila, come in. Sit." Mrs. Derby motioned for Jeremy to bring the extra chair from the corner.

Jeremy set her chair next to his, away from the others.

"We were just saying we would very much appreciate hearing from you about the day you took off your burqa following the field hockey tryouts. This young man says Ester may have said something hurtful to you, and that he overheard something she said that he finds objectionable.

Can you elaborate?" She paused to allow Laila, or anyone else, to fill the void. "At all?"

They sat in silence. As they waited, Jeremy heard the clock ticking as loudly as his heart, which thumped in his ears, bringing intense heat with each beat. Mrs. Derby twisted her necklace absentmindedly with one hand, drumming her fingers on the desk with the other. At last, Laila said simply, "No."

Mrs. Derby trained her eyes on Laila, clearly expecting more. But more never came.

As Jeremy sat next to Laila, head low, he was strangely transported to the candle-lit silence of church. On Christmas Eve, just before the midnight candles were lit, that frozen moment in time before the pastor announced, "Rejoice he has come …" That sleepy moment that felt like an exclamation point at the end of a busy, harried day with relatives and neighbors and family expecting help in the kitchen … It was a solemn silence. Like they were suddenly on holy ground.

Mina and Laila sat unmoving, unreadable. Susan continued her blank stare at the wall. Angela gazed uselessly at a point on the desk between her and Mrs. Derby.

It was Ester, whose hands had gone still as Laila entered the room, who broke the silence. "I was trying to help." She looked over at Laila apologetically. "You were doing so well. I have never seen anyone get to the places on the field they need to be so fast. But you couldn't see the passes in time. Because of the veil." She brushed something invisible off her lap. "I didn't mean to upset you."

Susan, still in her wall-gazing trance, said, "Trying to help. That's all. Just trying to help."

Mrs. Derby placed her palms on her desk. "Well," she said. "Thank you for clarifying, Ester. Is there anything you'd like to add, Laila?"

Laila's head was still bowed. She and her mother turned to each other for a moment and locked their screened eyes. Laila shook her head.

Mina said, "I like your idea, Mrs. Derby, of a student-led educational program." Mrs. Derby nodded. "I wonder if part of the program could include something about the Muslim ways. To prevent misunderstandings."

"Religious tolerance would certainly be part of such a program. *But.* We can't be seen as advocating one religion over another. Or excluding other faith-based beliefs."

Angela turned to Jeremy. "You wanted to help Laila. This sounds like a way to help her as well as others."

Jeremy felt a pain in his stomach as the tide turned toward action of a kind he hadn't set out for. "Fine," he said, fighting the impulse to argue. "If Ester and Laila do it with me."

He could barely concentrate as Mrs. Derby explained the program and emailed the materials to the three of them. A date was set on the school calendar, and Ester was invited back to school. As they left the office, Jeremy turned to Laila. "Can I walk you to your class?"

"I'd like that," she said.

Angela gave Jeremy's arm a squeeze; he knew she wanted

to hug him and appreciated her effort to refrain. There was immense pride on her face. He said, "See you at home."

Ester shoved Jeremy playfully as she passed in the hallway.

Susan drifted past without acknowledging either of them.

"Is she always like that?" Jeremy asked his mother.

"Hmm. No," Angela said. "Have a good rest of the day. I'm going to see what's up with her." She patted Jeremy on the shoulder and followed Susan out the door.

Mina was the last one out of the office."Nice to meet you, Jeremy."

"Nice to meet you as well, Mrs. Haver."

"Call me Mina." Then she said to Laila, "Where were you all morning?"

"Prayers," Laila whispered.

Mina nodded. The two of them looked up at the school clock and then at each other. An acknowledgment passed between them. "You'll be going to classes now, right?"

"Right." Mina hugged her daughter and left.

As they walked to class, Jeremy felt the stares of students passing by. He didn't care. He wanted to reach for Laila's hand but there was so much he didn't know. "I'm glad you came," he said.

"Thanks. It wasn't easy."

"So it's back to the burqa?"

She shoved him the way she saw Ester do it. "I may go shopping for head scarves," she said. She touched the edge of her hood. "This one's getting old."

chapter

30

ANGELA SPOTTED SUSAN ACROSS THE PARKING LOT AND CALLED, "WAIT UP!" Susan turned, but the vacant expression remained. "That went well, right?" Angela said once she'd caught up.

Susan nodded.

"I mean, the kids all seemed fine with the resolution. Obviously, some parenting needs to happen at this point as well," Angela said in her best sage voice. She got no reply as she walked alongside Susan a few paces. Angela stopped in her tracks and huffed. "Okay, what's up?"

Before she could answer, Mina was behind them. "Hello, friends," she said.

"Oh, hi, Mina! I like that word. Friends." Angela beamed at them both. Then she turned serious. "Listen, I was just asking Susan what's up. You don't seem yourself, my friend." Yes, friend had a great ring to it.

"I'm not sure what's up," Susan said vaguely. "Or down, actually." Then a spark lit her face and she turned to Mina. "I am so sorry about the video, Mina. Have you seen it?"

"Oh my God, Jeremy just told me," Angela said. "I am so, so sorry, Mina!"

"Don't be," Mina said. "I have endured worse, believe me. It's just … well, Laila has had such a rough start to the year. I hope this doesn't cause her more problems."

"Oh, right," Angela said. "Well, I doubt Jeremy would say anything to anyone. Would Ester, you think?"

Susan shook her head. "I don't know quite what to think about Ester's actions these days," she said.

"Right. Well, can I give you guys a ride home?" Angela was eager to change the subject. "We need to plan our next run, don't we?"

"We should talk about that," Mina said. "I took the bus, so a ride would be appreciated. Thank you, Angela."

"No problem. Let me drive you too, Susan. Can Ester take the car home?"

Susan looked a bit startled by the question, then relieved. "Yes, good idea. I think she has my keys, actually."

As Angela led them to her car, she said to Mina. "You and I never told each other our stories."

"Our what?" Mina said.

"Remember? The day I met you, I rambled on and on about being an American transplant and said I wanted to know about your Syrian journey. You said you wanted to hear about my story too, but you were probably just being nice." Before Mina could answer, she added, "I confess I know zero about your culture and the Muslim religion in general." They arrived at her car and Angela unlocked the doors. "I don't want to pry, though." she said.

Mina opened the back door for Susan and got in the front seat. "Yes, I would like that. Maybe we could share stories on our next run."

The two of them noticed Susan was still standing outside the car next to the open door. Angela gave Mina a puzzled look. She got out and saw Susan staring up at the trees, watching birds flit about in the branches. "Earth to Susan?" Angela said.

Susan smiled vaguely. "Sad, isn't it? The birds have to change. They can't just pick a place to live and settle in. Always changing."

Angela scanned Susan appraisingly. Her hair had tangles in it. Did her skin seem a bit gray? Maybe it was the light. But her eyes were distant and unfocused, and though Angela didn't know Susan that well yet, something about her was off.

"Are you on drugs?" Angela asked across the top of the car.

"Oh no!" Mina said from inside the car. Susan slid into

the back seat, giving Angela no choice but to duck in the driver side.

"Something wrong?" Susan saw Mina had her phone out.

"Not wrong, but I forgot I have an appointment today. Can you drop me off, Angela?"

"Of course, where?"

"It's not too far from the ShapeShifters office, actually," Mina said. "If you head that way, I can direct you."

"Okay, no problem." Angela started the car. "Susan, where do you live?"

"Also in that neighborhood," Susan said. "Drop Mina first since she has time constraints, and then I'll direct you."

Angela hesitated, assessing Susan once more. She was staring at the birds again from her window. Angela smiled at Mina, shrugging her shoulders and pulling out of her parking spot. "So …" Angela glanced back at Susan, who was out of bird-watching range.

"I'm not on drugs," Susan said, rolling her eyes. "I guess I'm not myself though. Feeling a bit rudderless, actually. Not sure why."

"Maybe running would help?" Mina said. "When is training number three?"

Susan slumped a little in her seat. "There's a bit of a snag."

"What's the snag?" Angela said. "Are you not allowed to train us since you don't work there anymore?"

"What do you mean she doesn't work there?" Mina said.

Susan made a motion like she was batting away a fly.

"Psssh … I'm sure that's temporary. I'm just waiting for Marty to come to his senses."

Mina turned to address Susan. "I am so sorry. I didn't know you were fired."

Susan jolted her head back like she'd been shot. "Not fired. Well, I don't know what's happening." She gazed out the window, her eyes drifting upwards. Angela wondered if she was looking for birds again. "First this thing with Ester," she said. "She's been a bit off, herself. I suppose I shouldn't be surprised she's been as insensitive at school as she's been toward me."

"That's a teenager thing," Angela said to the rearview mirror.

"Yeah, that's what I thought too." Susan let her eyes find the clouds again. "Lex, that's my husband, he works a lot. Ester is always busy. It's just me puttering about in the house most of the time. And now with this job hiatus, it's brought up … all these feelings." She said all this in a dreamy voice, gazing up at the sky. "I'm not sure what my role is in this world. Does that sound melancholy?" She touched a spot on the window. "I'm adrift right now. Don't know where I'll land."

Mina turned around again to look at Susan. "Well, one of your roles is to help us become runners, isn't it?"

Susan smiled. "How about tomorrow?" she said. "We can meet at my house. There are some good paths around there."

"Works for me," Angela said.

"Me too," said Mina. "Just turn down that street right

there," she instructed Angela. After Angela turned, there were two more turns in short succession before Mina told her to stop.

"What appointment is this?" Susan asked, scanning the row of duplexes in front of them suspiciously.

"I'll have to tell you all about it another time," Mina said, pulling her sleeve back to check her watch. "I'm basically helping out this kind old woman. Do you guys have a chess game by chance?"

"I do," Susan said. "Why?"

"Well, she promised to teach me chess if I can find a board. Laila is interested in the game. I want to learn it so I can help her."

"Uh huh," Susan said, distractedly. "What's the woman's name?"

"I call her Mrs. Kelly," Mina said.

As Mina got out, Angela glanced at Susan. Her grayish face had gone ghostly white. "You okay?" she asked Susan.

Susan rolled down her window. "It's not Kelly Margaret, is it?" she asked Mina.

"I don't know. I'll ask. Bye, you guys. See you tomorrow. What's your address, Susan?"

Susan said nothing, staring daggers into one of the duplexes.

"I'll drive you tomorrow!" Angela shouted after rolling down the window. "I'll know where she lives after I drive her home. How about we run at noon, and I'll pick you up at eleven thirty?"

"That will be fine. Thanks again," Mina said. She waved

to a stunned-looking Susan in the back seat and hustled off toward the complex sidewalk.

Angela started to do a U-turn but Susan said, "Wait!"

Angela put the car in park and studied Susan, who was tracking Mina's progress. "Checking to make sure she gets in safely?"

Susan didn't answer. Once Mina found the right door, she walked up to the steps and raised her hand to knock. Before she could, the door flung open, briefly revealing an older woman who grabbed Mina's arm and hustled her inside.

"All good?" Angela said to Susan. But Susan looked too shocked to answer.

chapter

31

ANGELA WAS EXCITED FOR THE RUN WHEN SHE SHOWED UP WITH MINA AT SUSAN'S HOUSE. She was feeling stronger and lighter on her feet than last time.

Susan was slow to answer the door, so Angela confirmed she had the right address. Then she knocked, rang the doorbell, and repeated.

Eventually, Susan answered, looking more bedraggled than last time. A shocking mass of tangles framed her face. She was still wearing a vacant expression. Even more concerning, she was not dressed to run.

"Why are you still in your robe?" Angela said.

Susan followed Angela's eyes to her garb. "My housecoat?" Noticing Angela's car in her driveway, she added, "It's morning."

"It's lunch time, Susan." Mina said, her concern palpable.

Once inside, Angela detected a faint aroma of cinnamon. The sun-streaked marble floor yielded to a closet overflowing with sweaters, jackets, boots, and scarves. Crumpled papers spilled from the adjacent office, where folders and Post-its littered the desk top.

"You came for lunch?" Susan had one hand on her head, working distractedly at a coil of frizz.

"Alright, sleepy Susie." Angela took charge. "Get your running clothes on. Time to charge your batteries."

"Oh. Right." Susan widened her eyes. "That's today, isn't it?" She patted the sides of her hips as if realizing she wasn't dressed. "I'll go change."

Angela and Mina exchanged baffled looks and followed her up a circular staircase. With some prompting and investigating, they managed to locate running tights, an athletic bra, and a long-sleeved running hoodie. They ushered her outside before she could zone out again.

"What's the running plan?" Mina asked.

"The plan. Yes. Okay." Susan's eyes were tracking again. "Let's do a slow jog to warm up toward the park path."

They passed a few houses structured just like Susan's except with different brick, roof, or window treatments. Then they followed a playground path opening up to a green space where a woman was throwing a ball for her dog. "Let's stand in a little circle here to stretch," Susan said when they reached a fence. Beyond that, the path disappeared into a grove of trees.

As they mimicked Susan's movements, Mina tentatively suggested, "You still seem a little rudderless, Susan."

Susan extended her fingers above her head and reached toward the sky. Angela and Mina did the same. "Yep. Don't know whether I'm coming or going it seems," she said, and stretched her arms over to one side. "How was your visit with Mags? I mean, Kelly?"

"She was very tired yesterday," Mina said.

Susan touched her toes and bounced a little. The other two followed, Mina's sleeves now over her hands, lightly brushing the grass.

"I asked her if she knew you. She said yes."

Susan bolted upright. "What else did she say?"

"Not much else. Like I said, she was tired and wanted to nap sooner rather than later. We didn't even get to play a game. How do you know her?"

"She's my aunt. She doesn't like me much," Susan said.

A small orange ball plopped between them and the dog's owner said sorry, scooping it up, her dog flopping about wildly until she threw it again.

"Let's run, ladies," Susan said, heading off toward the forest path.

Mina scooped up her skirts and rushed ahead. "Why doesn't she like you?" she asked Susan.

"She thinks I took something that belongs to her."

"Did you?" Mina said, panting already.

"No."

Angela caught up just then. "What is the plan, exactly?" She paused to catch her breath.

"We are ready for 4k now, I think," Susan said. "We're just going to do a big loop here that I know is 4k. On the last half of the loop, we will pick up the pace, alternating every minute, to work on our fast-twitch muscles."

"I feel bad that Jo and Belinda aren't here," Angela said, her breath still uneven. She was longing for more distractions.

"Hmm, good point." Susan scratched her head, then took a moment to tie her hair up into a ponytail as they ran. "In case I'm not back at the meeting next week, can you guys get their contact info so I can invite them to join us?"

"For sure," Angela said brightly. She focused on her breath for a few paces and felt a bit better.

Mina panted quietly beside them.

"So. Have you heard anything from Marty about coming back?"

"Not yet. Why?"

"Maybe you should contact him. You know. To clarify."

Susan sped up a little and Angela left Mina at the slower pace, sidling up to Susan. "I mean, he had a replacement at the meeting. So …"

Susan stopped, glaring. "What are you driving at, Angela?"

Mina caught up to them, wheezing from the effort.

"Okay, hear me out," Angela said. "You're a bit of a wreck, no offense."

Susan glared harder.

"Sorry, but you said yourself you feel rudderless."

Susan huffed and started jogging again. The other two fell in beside her.

"Isn't it possible you are in denial about being"—Angela cleared her throat—"fired?"

Susan stopped again. Mina had dropped behind. "I. Wasn't. Fired."

"Okay. And if that's the case, why are you drifting about in robes—"

"—housecoat."

"Why are you drifting about with tangled, unwashed hair, in your housecoat, with cookie crumbs on you?" Angela brushed something off Susan's temple.

Mina caught up again. She breathed slowly in and out, her hands on her knees.

"I am an exemplary employee," Susan said. "I was supposed to be a teacher but I gave that all up for my kids. This was the only job I could find part-time that worked for my family, and I am fucking overqualified for it!" Susan's eyes welled up with tears. She started running again, batting at her eyes.

Angela and Mina stuck close to her heels.

"Once the kids were out," Susan yelled back at them, "I was going to be promoted. I was gunning for management. And Marty gave me every reason to believe I was the top candidate." She wiped something off her nose. "Being fired from my low-wage filler-job is *not* in the plan." Susan let out a little sob. Punctuating each step, she yelled out, "I can't be a teacher. I can't be a weight-loss specialist. Where does that leave me? Who will I see … When I look in the mirror?"

They plodded along, letting Susan's little crisis wash over them. They passed another dog with its owner, then a small pond.

Mina exclaimed, "Mirror! Kelly thinks you took a mirror."

Panting heavily, Angela blurted, "When is our walk break?"

chapter

32

BY WAY OF ANSWER, SUSAN RAN FASTER.

They arrived back at the house, breathless. Angela and Mina acted like they lost a lung, but Susan had to admit, she worked them pretty hard.

She had planned the pick-ups but once the mirror issue came up, she took flight. She was not sure why. The fight or flight response drove her to take off, and the other two had to work too hard to keep up. No talking possible. She felt more focused now, standing on her front porch, watching the two of them bent over in an effort to breathe. She was grateful for the adrenaline rush. Her heart was suddenly and inexplicably full of affection for these two people who, despite pushing her buttons, pushed her out the door as well.

Who else would have rescued her from her slump? Lex had a grueling schedule and he seemed to be home less and less now that the older kids were off on their own. Ester didn't even say good morning when she banged around downstairs, checking closets for sports paraphernalia and assembling her lunch from Tupperware in the fridge. Susan could sleep all day and no one would notice.

She led these two friends—yes she could call them friends for sure now—through a cool-down and stretching routine. And as they started breathing normally again, she began to worry they would harp on the mirror thing or the Marty thing again. Those were topics she had been avoiding. She realized she had avoided the mirror issue for years. And Marty. Well, he should have had her back. Angela was right. She needed to take action. Not just wait for things to work out for her somehow.

Before either one could bring it up again, Susan admitted, "I did take the mirror, but it belonged to my dad, not Mags. My aunt is a bit nuts about that mirror." She waggled a finger by her ear. "It makes her so crazy. I just never confessed to having it."

"I can see why you might be concerned for her mental health," Mina said. "She thinks it has magic powers or something."

Because it does, Susan thought. She turned to unlock the door, pulling a key from the pocket of her tights. She unlocked the door quickly and waved them inside.

"So. *Does* it have magical powers?" Angela persisted.

Susan didn't answer right away. Now that she'd admitted having the mirror and her beef with Marty, her demons bumped around in her head, demanding attention. She slipped off her shoes. Dropping her key on the table by the stairs, she tried to focus on the thoughts now crystallizing in her brain. "It does for me." It was her best answer. It was the truth.

"Well, let's see it then," Angela said.

Mina shook her head. "I don't like how this feels." She aimed a scolding finger at Susan. "You took something Kelly thinks belongs to her, you denied having it, you both think it is magic. This is twisted." She turned to Angela. "We should not be involved."

"Oh come on! At least tell us what's so *magical*," Angela said, using air quotes.

"Tell you what." Susan patted her stomach. "I'm starving. Can't remember the last time I ate, actually. Let's have some lunch and I'll think about it."

Angela's stomach growled, making the three laugh. "Lunch sounds like a plan." Angela smiled gratefully.

They took off their running jackets and followed Susan to the kitchen. She opened the fridge and considered the contents. "What do you guys usually have for lunch?"

"The smoothies have been great," Angela said, "but I could use something a bit more substantial today."

"Fair enough." Susan looked at Mina questioningly.

"I haven't been eating lunch."

"What? Why?"

"I don't know what I can eat from my traditional recipes

and still lose weight. So I have fruit and yogurt for breakfast. No lunch. And a small portion of whatever I prepare for dinner."

Mina explained what went into her traditional meals, and though some of the ingredients weren't familiar to Susan, she could see there were a lot of starches and fats in the recipes.

Fetching an egg carton from the fridge's depths, Susan asked, "Do you eat eggs?"

"Yes."

Susan set the eggs on the counter. "How about peas?"

"Yes."

"Okay, ladies, I'm going to whip up some scrambled eggs with peas for lunch. Plus"—she checked her veggie drawers, which were virtually empty—"pumpkin bread." She took out a can of puréed pumpkin from her pantry and waved it like a flag.

"I must be really hungry," Angela said, "because my mouth is watering over peas, pumpkin, and eggs?"

"You're going to love it!" Susan laughed, explaining how easy pumpkin bread was to make and emphasizing how filling ingredients led to satisfaction, whereas sugar created uncontrolled binging behavior. She took out a bottle of agave syrup and a mixing bowl. "You guys can help."

An hour later, they sat in Susan's brightly-lit dining room to eat. Susan removed a chunky, ornate candelabra from the middle of the round table so they could see each other. Whenever she sank into the high-back purple velvet chairs flecked with gold on the edges, she wished she ate in that room more often. The windows by the table overlooked a small, overgrown backyard. Since fall had arrived, her shrubs and trees were so vibrant the yard looked perfectly manicured. And the occasional appearance of bunnies allowed her to continue the family tradition of leaving carrots on the back steps. It started as a winter practice, but she couldn't help doing it year-round.

"Why do eggs and peas taste so good?" Angela scooped up the last yellow mound with her fork and chased a couple of stray peas on her plate.

"Lucky for me, you're hungry," Susan laughed. "It's all I could come up with that might work for Mina."

Mina had taken off her head coverings to eat. It was the first time they had seen her face. She was strikingly beautiful, her dark glossy hair flecked with gray and tied back in braids. Her sparsely wrinkled face and resolute jawline reflected wisdom and kindness, plus unknown worlds of pain. She nodded agreeably, her mouth full, her plate almost empty.

"Canned peas add the requisite salty taste," Susan said. "Makes you forget there's virtually no fat in it."

"This recipe should go in your file," Angela said, finishing the last of her pumpkin bread. "After you give it to me, of course!"

Susan smiled, making no effort to hide her pleasure. She had added the mashed banana last minute in case the agave wasn't enough to sweeten the pumpkin. "It has no sugar in it, and lots of healthy fats," she said proudly.

"Have you thought any more about making a cookbook?"

"A little. I renamed my recipe file. Now that I don't have a job." Susan surprised herself by admitting this. The admission came with no sting. "I have no members to create recipes for. So what's the point?"

"The point?" Mina touched her lips with a napkin. "You created this for me, your friend. Not Mina the member."

"Yeah," Angela said. "All the members you've cooked up recipes for over the years. They are just a reflection of others out there, waiting for a cookbook like yours!"

"Thank you, guys. Maybe this is the kick in the pants I need to move forward." Susan stood up and collected plates. Mina and Angela followed her to the kitchen with glasses and the empty bread tin.

"I hate to infringe on your time," Mina said, "but could I have a look at your chess game?"

"Of course! I'll give you a quick lesson. Do you play, Angela?"

"Not in years. I lack that whole planning-two-steps-ahead quality when it comes to strategic games."

"Oh gosh. Let's not worry about that," Susan said. "We'll walk through the basics today. Leave the strategizing for the professionals."

Susan showed Mina how to set up the board and how each piece moved. The inside of the box had diagrams that helped Mina remember. They played a game with Angela and Mina alternating turns on the one side, so everyone could play. An hour passed quickly.

When Susan caught Angela looking at her watch, she

realized school would be out soon. "I guess we will have to reconvene another time."

"Same time next week?" Angela hopped a little. "I can bring lunch."

Mina did a little dance too, waiting for Susan's answer.

Susan beamed. "Yes, let's do that. But please let me know Belinda's and Jo's contact information so I can include them."

They followed Susan to the office near the foyer and waited while she slid the chess box into a drawer.

"So about that mirror …" Angela lingered by the front door. "You said you'd think about it over lunch?"

Mina peered anxiously at the door, which Angela was blocking. She quickly reassembled her running shirt and scarves while Angela awaited Susan's response.

Susan let the voices in her head hash it out for a few moments. *It's not really magic*, she reminded herself. *What's the harm?*

It's magic for you, came an answering thought. *As long as you wonder, you keep the amazing stories Dad told you alive.*

I can keep them alive regardless of the mirror's magic, she reassured herself.

Aware of Angela's expectant, pleading expression, she sighed. "I'm sorry. I'm not ready."

Angela nodded. Even through the veil, Susan felt Mina's tension dissipate.

Angela slid on her running jacket and the two of them laced up their runners. Mina had her hand on the door but stopped to say, "I'll be seeing Kelly on Tuesday. I'm sure she'd like to see you."

Susan felt a jolt of guilt. "I'll think about it. Okay?"

"Hey." Angela caught Mina's sleeve. "How do you know Kelly again?"

"My husband ran over her with his car." Mina laughed at the shock on their faces. "She's a tough lady," she added, opening the door. "Like you," she said to Susan.

After they left, Susan opened the desk drawer and touched the mirror to ensure it was there. She didn't want to see its clouded reflection. She was not ready for that. Before she could look at it again, before she could show it to others and tell them the story of her father, there was something she must do.

chapter

33

MINA WAS A BUNDLE OF NERVES ON THE BUS RIDE TO KELLY'S. She couldn't shake the feeling she was an imposter, naked and shameful. She reminded herself that unveiling her face was a choice. She checked off the reasons in her head. The same reasons she went over and over before she decided. Once she arrived on Kelly's step, she felt immense relief. Still, she was lost in a muddle of self-deprecation when the door swung open.

"Did you get my damn mirror back?" Kelly's eyes widened in disbelief. She wiped her fingers on a pink, ruffled apron, leaving dusty traces.

Mina giggled, pointing at the hand-embroidered lettering on the apron: Make It Yourself. "Well," Mina said, "What do you think?"

Kelly looked her up and down, then stepped back and assessed some more.

Mina shifted her weight from one foot to the other, hands on her hips.

"I knew you had nice eyes." Kelly clapped her hands, then waved her inside. "Come in, come in. Tell me why you've shown up in such a state."

Mina gratefully slipped out of her runners and put them on the rack. Once inside, she pulled off her running jacket and brought both hands to the sides of her head like she'd done a hundred times that day to make sure her scarf was snugly in place.

Kelly closed the door behind her. "Well?" she prompted.

Mina shrugged her shoulders. "If you ever tried to run in a burqa, you'd know why."

The kitchen smelled like apples and cardamom. Mina looked around. A board covered the top of the table where they usually sat. Bits of dough were gathered into a pile. Flour sprinkled the surface.

"You're early. I was just about to clean that up," Kelly said.

Mina retrieved a pastry cutter she saw drying next to the sink and handed it to Kelly. She pulled out the compost bin and held it under the table's edge. Kelly scraped the flour and doughy bits into the compost. "You worshipping the god of running now?" Kelly said as she scraped.

Mina replaced the compost bin under the sink. "It's not about worship."

"What's it about then?"

Mina grabbed the dishcloth and gave the board a good wipe. She glanced at Kelly, who was studying her headscarf. "It was time for a change." Together they picked up the heavy board and shuffled over to the counter where Kelly signaled they should put it down.

"Hmph," Kelly said. "What does your daughter think about it?"

Mina smiled conspiratorially. "She doesn't know yet."

The oven buzzed. Kelly punched the timer button and opened the oven. Using mitts slung on the counter, she took out a pie, letting loose an intense aroma Mina could almost taste. Kelly sat the pie on a stove burner to cool. Then she poured two cups of coffee and gestured for Mina to sit.

Mina moved chairs from the wall beneath the clock to the small table and sat in one, blowing on the coffee Kelly set on the table in front of her. "You are moving quite well now," Mina said. "How are your knees?"

Kelly's eyebrows knitted themselves into a frown. "Never you mind that. It comes and goes, my knee troubles. Having a good day is all."

Mina smiled. "I like visiting with you. I'm not going to stop because your knees are better."

"Do what you want," Kelly said. "Are you going to have some pie or are you still on a diet?"

Mina was tempted. She thought about her goal of another pound this week. And the run. Then she realized she forgot to make herself lunch before she came. "Maybe just a sliver."

Kelly nodded approvingly. "How's your daughter?"

Mina's eyes brightened. "She is well, thank you. All A's so far."

"Well, you're doing something right, then. And the mirror? Did you ask my no-account niece about my mirror?"

"I don't want to be involved in that witchcraft," Mina said, severely. "I told you that's between you and Susan."

Kelly scoffed then stood to check on the pie.

"Worldly things should not get in the way of family," Mina added.

Kelly placed her hands on either side of the stove and sighed. "If you're done lecturing me, maybe you could tell me how she's doing," she said to the pie.

Mina got up and placed a comforting hand on Kelly's shoulder. "She's had a tough week or two. Her daughter gives her some trouble, she got fired from the weight clinic …" Kelly straightened at this and turned around to face Mina. "And she seems a bit lonely with Ester so busy and Lex working so much."

"Why on earth is he working so much? This should be their time now, with kids in transition."

Mina shrugged. "You should ask her."

Kelly opened a drawer and found a knife and a pie spatula. Mina took out two plates from the cabinets above. "Oh! She taught me how to play chess. Sort of."

Kelly looked impressed. "That so?"

There was a firm rapping at the door that made them

both jump. Mina looked at the clock. "Oh dear. It's time for the run."

"The what?" Kelly eyed her warily as she headed for the door.

"We're doing our training run from—" Before Mina could finish, Kelly thrusted open the door, revealing her niece, who was holding a brightly colored gift bag. Pink polka dots decorated the bag and delicate pink tissue stuck out of it.

"Hi, Aunt Mags." Susan kissed her stunned aunt on the cheek. Then she stepped back and waited patiently while Kelly looked her up and down, mouth agape. "It's a peace offering." Susan handed over the gift bag. "For being a terrible niece who considers herself too busy to visit her favorite aunt."

"I'm your only aunt." Kelly stood aside so Susan could come in.

"Wow, smells great in here." Susan said. She set a cloth shopping bag on the floor by her shoes. "Is that cardamom I smell?"

"We were about to have some apple pie," Kelly said. "Suppose it's okay for you to join us if you want."

Susan smiled apologetically, about to decline. But she was interrupted by another knock at the door.

"My word," Kelly said. "Does the whole world know I made pie?" She opened the door to three strangers on her step peering at her quizzically.

"Is this the right place?" Jo had her arms folded over her ski jacket.

"Mags, these are my friends, Jo, Angela, and Belinda." Susan pointed at each one in turn. "Guys, this is my beloved Mags."

"Oh, for Chrissakes," Kelly said.

"Sorry to bother you." Belinda bounced a little on the step. "Did Susan tell you we were meeting here?"

"No, she did not," Kelly said. "I suppose you will all want pie, then."

"Thanks, Mags, but we have to get through a run. The pie might weigh us down," Susan said. Jo rubbed her stomach mournfully as it emitted an audible gurgle.

"Woah, look at you," Belinda said, taking in Mina's new look. "Sporty spice!"

Mina blushed and tucked an imaginary hair into her headscarf. "Experimenting with running wear." Mina winked a shiny brown eye. "I can't be tripping on the race course, can I?"

Jo gave her the thumbs-up. "All. Right!"

"Okay then, off you go if you're going to turn down my hospitality." Kelly shooed them toward the open door.

"Another time?" Jo said, hopefully.

"What's in the bag?" Belinda asked.

All eyes turned to the pretty little gift bag on the table. Susan's panicked eyes met Kelly's, whose eyebrows shot up. Susan scrambled. "Let's go, runner friends. Mags can open that on her own time …"

Before she could finish her sentence, Kelly had yanked the tissue paper with one hand and scooped out the contents with the other. In her hand gleamed a fake-jeweled mirror like something you'd find in a dollar store. Kelly turned the mirror around in her hands and smiled with satisfaction.

"Finally!" she said, holding the mirror up by its handle for all to see. It was shaped like a pingpong paddle

Mina tried to avert her eyes and inch toward the door but couldn't help noticing the filmy nature of the mirror-side.

"It's okay, Mina. It doesn't reflect anything," Angela said.

Mina peered into it tentatively like it might be a dangerous, sleeping creature. She saw the olive oval of her face, warped and unrecognizable.

Kelly handed it to her. "Isn't it amazing?"

One by one, they passed around the mirror, gathering around Kelly like a prayer circle.

When it got to Belinda, she seemed perplexed. "It doesn't reflect anything."

"Well, it's probably old," Jo offered.

"It is," Kelly said to Jo, eyes glistening. "It has changed over time. It reveals less and less as time goes on. But back in the day …"

"It was magic," Susan finished, her eyes fixed in the air above the mirror, her whispery voice sad and resigned.

Susan blinked, coming back to the present, and reached for the bag she had set by her shoes. "I almost forgot!" She reached in with both arms and pulled out a stack of books. "I'm published," she said, passing the books around to everyone.

Angela jumped up and down and hugged Susan. "The cookbook! You did it!" She flipped through the pages, calling out the recipes that excited her.

"The Crave-Killer Cookies!" Belinda squealed.

"I love the cover," Jo said. It was a cheery green color with white lettering in a simple font. "It's Not Complicated," she read. "By Susan Snow."

"Look at the back," Susan said.

"Dedicated to my dear friends: Angela, Mina, Belinda, and Jo," Mina read.

"I credit you for some of the recipes," she told Kelly, who grinned awkwardly, absentmindedly wiping her clean fingers on her apron.

"The next version will have a picture of us finishing the race," Susan added, pointing to the large blank space under her dedication.

They spent some time chatting excitedly about the race and picking out recipes they wanted to try, until Susan said, "Okay, let's run, ladies!"

After the cookbooks were safely stowed in their cars and Kelly had said her goodbyes to each of them, urging them to not be strangers, they followed Susan down the sidewalk toward the park. Mina detected a little extra spring in their steps.

chapter 34

ANGELA SAT ON THE SECOND-FLOOR BALCONY WITH MELVIN SIPPING GREEN TEA, A GIGANTIC BOWL OF CANDY WAITING IN THE FOYER ONE FLOOR BELOW FOR THE ONSLAUGHT OF TRICK-OR-TREATERS.

"You sure you don't want a beer? Glass of wine?" Melvin said.

Angela shook her head. "Can't risk being weak around candy."

They heard some shuffling on the sidewalk. Melvin looked at his watch and raised his eyebrows at Angela. It was only 4:00 p.m. They peered over the glass banister. Jeremy was on the sidewalk below, chatting animatedly with two other girls.

"That's Laila. And Ester." Angela scratched her head. "You know, from the school debacle? Their moms are my friends?"

"Ah," Melvin said. He rose to bring his cup to the kitchen. Angela downed her last sip of tea as Mel surveyed his options in the beer fridge.

The doors downstairs banged open, followed by some excitement over the bowl of candy. "That's for the trick-or-treaters!" Angela called downstairs.

Moments later, the three teenagers ascended the stairs to the kitchen floor. "Hi, Mom." Jeremy had a new ease about his actions. *More like his old self*, Angela thought. "You know Ester and Laila, right?"

Angela tried to keep a straight face but she could have burst with joy, seeing Jeremy with friends. "Of course! Good to see you again." She casually rinsed out her cup, reminding herself not to over-enthuse. "You guys going out for Halloween?"

"Mom, we're too old for that." Although Jeremy rolled his eyes good-naturedly, the girls stared at their shoes. Angela thought they seemed disappointed.

Laila wore jeans and a V-neck sweater. A loose green scarf around her neck brought out a glossiness in her jet black hair that hung in waves to her waist.

"I see." Angela winked at the girls. "Well. How about I save some of the best chocolate for you then?" They smiled and nodded. "So you're not trick-or-treating. Are you studying?"

"Nah. We're helping Ester with that seminar the principal wants her to do."

Angela couldn't have felt more proud of Jeremy at that moment. Her heart fluttered in her chest like it had wings.

Melvin appeared from behind her with a beer and frosted glass. "What kind of seminar? Can I help?"

Angela introduced the teenagers to Melvin, who shook their hands before returning to his beer-pouring.

"Thanks for the offer," Jeremy said after the introductions. "We'll let you know when we figure out what we're doing."

"Laila, I hope you don't mind my saying," Angela said, "I love that outfit on you. Your eyes remind me of your mother's."

"Thanks." Laila's cheeks flushed pink.

"I'm trying to talk her into joining the field hockey team," Ester said.

"Wow. That's great."

Laila shot Ester an admonishing look. "I said I'd think about it." Then she explained to Angela, "Thought she could use my help on the seminar though. And we dragged Jeremy into it too!"

It was Jeremy's turn to blush. "Now you've thrown chocolate at us, I may never get out of this seminar thing. Let's work downstairs," he said to the girls. "I have a table in my room we can fit around." He turned back toward the stairs and the other two followed. Angela noticed Laila touch his sleeve as they climbed the steps.

chapter 35

SUSAN PLACED THE CHICKEN AND POTATOES INTO THE OVEN AND SET THE TIMER. This was her first stab at Syrian cooking and so far she was pleased. The chicken fell apart nicely after boiling. And prepping the potatoes took no time at all. As the aroma of garlic filled the kitchen, she was grateful she took the time to mash the cloves with a hammer on the cutting board rather than cheating with the minced garlic in a jar.

She checked her phone. Twenty minutes until her guests would arrive. Perfect. From the fridge, she took out the green pepper, tomato, cucumber, lemon, mint, and parsley.

She was halfway through dicing the vegetables when her phone rang. *It must be Lex.* He hadn't come home the night before, which was not unusual, but she had no idea when to expect him, and she wanted to warn him about her impromptu celebration party.

She wiped her hands on the dish cloth and checked her phone. It was Marty, not Lex. Taking a moment to breathe, she was tempted to ignore it. *Might as well get it over with, whatever his problem is now*, she decided.

"Hi, Marty." Her voice was terse, efficient. "What's up?" She sauntered over to the picture window and surveyed the backyard. The flowers had all dried up and dropped to the earth. The pile of leaves she raked yesterday was still there. A bunny nibbled leisurely at a carrot she had thrown out the door that morning.

"Glad I caught you," Marty said. "How are you doing, Susan?" His voice was congenial. Not what she expected.

"You mean since you fired me? Quite well, no thanks to you," Susan said, savoring the confidence she felt now.

"Fired?" Marty said. "Yes, I guess I did say you're fired, didn't I? You should know better than to listen to my actual words by now, Susan." He forced out a laugh that fell flat.

Susan said nothing.

Marty cleared his throat. "Of course I didn't mean to fire you—you're the best in the district."

Susan wasn't buying it. "That's strange, because you've apparently replaced me at the meeting from what I understand."

"Right, right," Marty said. "Listen, I have something new for you. How would you like to be my assistant?"

"Assistant?"

"Yes, you know. Follow me around, learn the ropes, get some experience. There are some management positions opening up in Toronto. With your track record as a support leader and some shadowing experience, this opportunity could set you up nicely for applying—"

"You want me to be your assistant."

"Yes."

"After you fired me."

"Well, I'd like to make up for that. It was a rash decision on my part. Congratulations, by the way! That cookbook of yours keeps popping up everywhere. The *Globe and Mail* article was extremely complimentary."

"My cookbook was mentioned in the *Globe and Mail*?"

"You didn't see it? Well, I'll send you the link."

Susan waited as Marty tapped at his laptop. *Globe and Mail*, she repeated in her head, smiling proudly.

"I hear some of our members from your meeting bring up the recipes on a regular basis. Can't really blame them, but it's probably best to develop a collaborative effort on the project."

Susan's brain tripped over the word "collaborative."

"Otherwise, the powers that be might have to take a look at the Covenant Not to Compete Clause …"

"Let me get this straight," Susan said. "You fired me. Your members are crazy about my cookbook now. Suddenly, you want in on the action. And to sweeten the pot, you want to give me a promotion while threatening me with legal action if I don't credit ShapeShifters for my recipes?"

"*Threatening* is not the word I'd use …" Marty's voice was suddenly tinged with anger, all caramel-ly sweetness dissolved.

"Goodbye, Marty." Susan hung up the phone, chiding herself for answering in the first place. She gazed out the window for a few more seconds. The bunny had moved to the side yard, his fluff ball of a tail disappearing beneath the bush.

Marty called back immediately. She let it go to voice mail. She checked her email and saw he had forwarded the article from the Toronto paper. In her inbox was another unopened email. Clicking on it, she saw it was from a Canadian cookbook publisher. She skimmed the letter, heart thumping hard in her chest. It mentioned her book by name and asked for a meeting.

The doorbell rang. *Oh man*, Susan thought. *The salad!* She ran to the front door and opened it to find Mina, Angela, Jo, and Belinda beaming at her from the step.

"My God, it smells good in here!" Belinda said, stepping inside with the others, each stopping to give Susan a hug.

"I am still on a high," Mina said. "I can't believe I finished a 7k race!"

"That's just a start," Susan said. "You have all improved so much."

"Did you see this?" Jo said, plopping the Toronto paper into Susan's hands.

"No, but I heard about it," Susan said with a huge smile.

She couldn't hold back. She was positively beaming with excitement and felt like she might burst.

"Well, we have more orders for the book," Belinda said, handing Susan an envelope. "That's all cash. *And* about a hundred orders for more!"

"Oh my, you guys," Susan said. "Is this all from the members?"

"Members who told friends and family who told neighbors … My phone has been ringing off the hook," Belinda said. "I should have given them your number!"

"Yeah," Jo said. "And I gave a copy to my boss. Did you know I work for a publishing company?"

Susan jumped with excitement. "What?"

"Relax. It's a textbook company. But my boss has been making the recipes and loves them. She mentioned it to some people she knows in the industry. I wouldn't be surprised if someone contacts you—"

"I have an email!" Susan said.

The oven timer went off just then. "The chicken and potatoes. The salad!" Susan rushed away toward the kitchen. "Throw your coats in the closet and come help me chop," she bellowed. "I'm going to need some sous chefs!"

THE END

The It's-Not-Complicated Cookbook

BY SUSAN SNOW

Ba-Na-No-Sugar Bread

Ingredients

- 1/2 C. almond flour
- 1/2 C. coconut flour
- 1 Tbs. tapioca starch
- 1 1/4 tsp. baking soda
- 1/2 tsp. salt
- 1/2 tsp. vanilla extract
- 2 Tbs. coconut oil
- 4 eggs
- 3 ripe bananas
- 1/3 C. cacao nibs

Directions

Preheat oven to 350 F. Spray 9" x 5" loaf pan with cooking spray or use coconut oil.

In mixer, blend bananas until liquid. Then add eggs, vanilla and coconut oil. Mix well.

Add dry ingredients next, stirring slowly in mixer, then folding with a spatula.

Fold in cacao nibs. Dump the mixture into a loaf pan.

Cook for 40-45 minutes. Let cool, and voila! (When cool, I slide a knife around the edges to loosen, then turn the pan over to plop the loaf onto a cutting board.)

Perfect Goo-To-Crunch Ratio Nachos

Ingredients

- 16-20 tortilla chips
- 3 Tbs. finely chopped onion
- 3 Tbs. finely chopped jalapeño peppers
- 1/2 C. shredded mozzarella cheddar blend, Mexican spiced if available
- Sour cream, guacamole, hot sauce to taste (optional)

Directions

Line a dinner plate with your favorite brand of tortilla chips. (Stick to types with minimal ingredients. Corn, healthy oil like canola or olive, and salt are all that's needed for taste and crunch.)

Chips can overlap but avoid big piles of chips. (The ones on the bottom may lose their crunch and get missed by the cheese!)

Sprinkle 3 Tbs. of finely chopped onion and 3 Tbsp. of finely chopped jalapeño pepper over top of the chips. (Jarred peppers are fine. If fresh, leave out the seeds to avoid spiciness overpowering the nachos.)

Spread 1-1/2 cups shredded Mexican mix cheese (or use equal parts mozzarella and cheddar) over top, making sure every chip gets some cheese coverage.

Place in microwave on high for approximately 1 minute. Serve with sour cream, guacamole, hot sauce and/or salsa of your choice.

Perfect goo-to-crunch ratio!

Three O'Clock Anti-Nappuccino Smoothie

Ingredients

- 1 C. unsweetened almond milk (or milk of your choice)
- 1 shot of espresso
- 1/2 C. frozen sliced strawberries
- 1 banana, sliced
- 1 tsp. all-natural peanut butter or cold-pressed olive oil (all bodies need a bit of oil, but too much will add up to extra pounds eventually)
- 1 tsp. powdered unsweetened cocoa

Directions

Add all ingredients to a blender and blend until smooth. Boom! Afternoon energy of a Frappuccino without the sugar crash.

Crave-Killer Cookies

The oats and peanut butter give these cookies the fiber and fat
necessary to cut short that must-eat-them-all-now temptation.

Ingredients

- 1-1/4 C. all purpose flour (or all-purpose gluten-free flour)
- 1 C. quick-cooking oats
- 1/2 tsp. each baking soda and salt
- 3/4 C. packed brown sugar
- 1/3 C. coconut oil or dairy butter
- 1/4 C. buttermilk (or place a few drops of lemon juice into 1/4 C. any type of milk)
- 1/3 C. mini chocolate chips (or chopped dark chocolate works great)

Directions

Preheat oven to 350 F. Spray cookie sheet with cooking spray
or use parchment paper.

In an electric mixer, whisk together wet ingredients until
well blended.

Dump the dry ingredients, except for chocolate chips, into
the blended wet ingredients, and blend together throughly.
Add the chocolate chips at the end and stir until evenly
distributed through the dough.

Roll dough into 1-1/2 inch balls and place them 2 inches apart on prepared cookie sheet. Using a fork dipped in flour, flatten the cookies to 1/4-inch thickness. Bake for 10 minutes (or less, depending on the oven. Don't overbake or the cookies will dry out).

Remove cookies from tray immediately and cool on a wire rack. Store in an airtight container.

To double the recipe, use only 2 cups of flour (not 1-1/2 cups). And use a little less than 2 cups of oats.

Pumpkin Maple Oat Scones

Ingredients

- 1 1/4 C. all purpose gluten-free flour
- 1/4 C. almond flour
- 1/4 C. oats
- 1/2 Tbs. baking powder
- 1 Tbs. brown sugar
- 1/4 tsp. salt
- 1 tsp. cinnamon mixed with ginger
- 1 stick cold butter, cubed
- 1/2 tsp. vanilla extract
- 1/4 C. pumpkin pureé
- 1 egg

Glaze:

- 1/2 C. powdered sugar
- 1/2 tsp. maple extract
- 1-2 Tbs. unsweetened almond milk

Directions

Preheat oven to 400 degrees F.

Add flour, oats, almond meal, baking powder, brown sugar, spice and salt to a food processor and process until well combined. Add butter and pulse until pea sized.

Transfer flour mixture to a large bowl. In a separate bowl, whisk together the almond milk, pumpkin pureé, egg and vanilla extract.

Add wet ingredients to the dry and mix until just combined.

Transfer to a floured surface, working with well-floured hands, and delicately pat into a 1-inch thick circle.

Cut into 8 even sections and transfer to a parchment-lined baking sheet. Bake for 20-22 minutes or until the bottoms are light golden brown and they look a little toasty on top.

Remove from the oven and let cool on a rack as you drizzle the glaze over top of the scones.

Acknowledgments

I owe a huge thank you to Carolyn Dittburner, who reached into my lonely world of self-editing and lent me her impressions. She asked probing questions and filled the margins of an early draft with jocular comments. Her input rescued me from an abyss of uncertainty.

Friend and former colleague, Leslie Mondle, quelled all remaining doubts when she gave me a richer perspective on Muslim customs. Her encouragement and reassurance brought me buckets of inner peace.

Monique Mensah of Make Your Mark Publishing Solutions seamlessly guided me through the professional editing process, patiently answered my countless questions, and skillfully managed the bones-to-book process. For all these reasons, not to mention her distinct brand of humor, I am exceedingly grateful.

Thank you for reading *The Shape of Us*
If you enjoyed this book, please leave an online review

KEEP IN TOUCH WITH MARY ANN TIPPETT
Website: www.maryanntippett.ca
Instagram: @maryanntippett
Twitter: @maryanntip

www.ingramcontent.com/pod-product-compliance
Lightning Source LLC
Chambersburg PA
CBHW030739110726
47900CB00008B/2369